P9-BEE-456

Praise for the first Candlemaking Mystery

At Wick's End

"A smashing, successful debut." —*Midwest Book Review*

"I greatly enjoyed this terrific mystery. The main character . . . will make you laugh. Don't miss this thrilling read."
—*Rendezvous*

"A clever and well-done debut." —*Mysterylovers.com*

Praise for
Tim Myers's Lighthouse Inn Mystery series

"A thoroughly delightful and original series. Book me at Hatteras West any day!" —Tamar Myers, author of *Gruel and Unusual Punishment*

"Myers cultivates the North Carolina scenery with aplomb and shows a flair for character."
—*Ft. Lauderdale Sun-Sentinel*

"Entertaining . . . authentic . . . fun . . . a wonderful regional mystery that will have readers rebooking for future stays at the Hatteras West Inn and Lighthouse." —*BookBrowser*

"Tim Myers proves that he is no one-book wonder. . . . A shrewdly crafted puzzle." —*Midwest Book Review*

"Colorful . . . picturesque . . . light and entertaining."
—Harriet Klausner

Lighthouse Inn Mysteries by Tim Myers

INNKEEPING WITH MURDER
RESERVATIONS FOR MURDER
MURDER CHECKS INN
ROOM FOR MURDER
BOOKED FOR MURDER

Candlemaking Mysteries by Tim Myers

AT WICK'S END
SNUFFED OUT

Snuffed Out

Tim Myers

BERKLEY PRIME CRIME, NEW YORK

THE BERKLEY PUBLISHING GROUP
Published by the Penguin Group
Penguin Group (USA) Inc.
375 Hudson Street, New York, New York 10014, U.S.A.
Penguin Group (Canada), 10 Alcorn Avenue, Toronto, Ontario, Canada M4V 3B2; (a division of Pearson Penguin Canada Inc.)
Penguin Books Ltd., 80 Strand, London WC2R 0RL, England
Penguin Group Ireland, 25 St. Stephen's Green, Dublin 2, Ireland (a division of Penguin Books, Ltd.)
Penguin Group (Australia), 250 Camberwell Road, Camberwell, Victoria 3124, Australia
(a division of Pearson Australia Group Pty., Ltd.)
Penguin Books India Pvt. Ltd., 11 Community Centre, Panchsheel Park, New Delhi—110 017, India
Penguin Group (NZ), Cnr. Airborne and Rosedale Roads, Albany, Auckland, New Zealand
(a division of Pearson New Zealand, Ltd.)
Penguin Books (South Africa) (Pty.) Ltd., 24 Sturdee Avenue, Rosebank, Johannesburg 2196, South Africa
Penguin Books Ltd., Registered Offices: 80 Strand, London, WC2R 0RL, England

This is a work of fiction. Names, characters, places, and incidents either are the product of the author's imagination or are used fictitiously, and any resemblance to actual persons, living or dead, business establishments, events, or locales is entirely coincidental.

SNUFFED OUT

A Berkley Prime Crime Book / published by arrangement with the author

PRINTING HISTORY
Berkley Prime Crime mass-market edition / December 2004

Copyright © 2004 by Tim Myers.
Cover design by George Long.
Cover illustration by Mary Anne Lasher.
Book design by Kristin del Rosario.

All rights reserved.
No part of this book may be reproduced, scanned, or distributed in any printed or electronic form without permission. Please do not participate in or encourage piracy of copyrighted materials in violation of the author's rights. Purchase only authorized editions.
For information, address: The Berkley Publishing Group, a division of Penguin Group (USA) Inc., 375 Hudson Street, New York, New York 10014.

ISBN: 0-425-19980-0

Berkley Prime Crime Books are published by The Berkley Publishing Group, a division of Penguin Group (USA) Inc., 375 Hudson Street, New York, New York 10014.
The name BERKLEY PRIME CRIME and the BERKLEY PRIME CRIME design are trademarks belonging to Penguin Group (USA) Inc.

PRINTED IN THE UNITED STATES OF AMERICA

10 9 8 7 6 5 4 3 2 1

If you purchased this book without a cover, you should be aware that this book is stolen property. It was reported as "unsold and destroyed" to the publisher, and neither the author nor the publisher has received any payment for this "stripped book."

*It's no mystery why this one's for
Patty and Emily.*

One

I was hunting for the short circuit that knocked out the power to River's Edge when I stumbled across Aaron Gaston's body. I hadn't known the potter all that well, exchanging a few greetings and a shared cup of coffee or two since I'd taken over the complex of small businesses from my Great-Aunt Belle. My candleshop, At Wick's End, was on the other side of the converted warehouse/factory from The Pot Shot, Aaron's name for his pottery studio. Still, I had no trouble identifying him in the weak beam of my flashlight as he lay sprawled on the floor in the middle of his studio. As the new owner of the building, I should have been more involved in my tenants' lives and businesses, but running the candleshop was nearly more than I could handle. I'd let Pearly Gray, my well-educated and erudite handyman, serve as my liaison to most of the folks who worked at River's Edge.

Now it appeared that I'd lost my last chance to get to know Aaron.

With a shaky hand, I reached for the telephone and

called Sheriff Morton. He was the final authority for the law in Micah's Ridge, at least as far as I was concerned.

"Morton here," he answered after the desk sergeant rang me through.

"I've got a problem," I said after identifying myself.

"Write a letter to Ask Ernestine," he said, "I've got my hands full right now."

I wasn't in the mood for his brusque manner. "Sheriff, one of my tenants is dead. I'm standing here in the dark with his body, and my flashlight's starting to flicker out."

That got his attention. "Sorry, Harrison, I've got three deputies out sick at the same time. There's a really nasty bug ripping through my department. Are you sure he's dead?"

I reluctantly trained the dimming beam over the body again. While dusk was just approaching outside, the shop was in near total darkness. There was still light enough from my flashlight to see the pallor of his face, though. Aaron was surrounded by a pool of darkness that I initially mistook for blood, but after a closer look, I could see that it was nothing more than spilled water. My imagination was definitely running on overtime.

"There's not much doubt about that," I said.

"Don't touch anything," Morton said, then added with a hint of chagrin in his voice, "You're using his phone, aren't you?"

"Yes, I grabbed his telephone. I had to call you, didn't I?"

After a sigh, Morton said, "Let me amend that, then. Don't touch anything else. And Harrison?"

"Yes?"

"I know it's not all that pleasant, but I'd appreciate it if you didn't leave the body until I got there."

After hanging up the phone, I stayed with Aaron about two seconds before I decided that staying with the body could mean a lot of different things. If I waited for Morton outside by the shop's front door, blocking the way of anyone else trying to get in, that should satisfy him.

It was going to have to, since my light was just about gone, and there was no way I was going to stand around in the dark with a dead body.

I used the master key Pearly had given me when we'd started checking on our tenants and locked the door behind me. I hadn't wanted to keep up with all those keys in the first place; there were over a dozen places of business at River's Edge, so I'd let Pearly watch after them for me. It was all I could do to keep with the keys to my apartment upstairs, both trucks, and of course, the ones for At Wick's End. Sometimes, particularly moments like the one I was experiencing, I'd wished my Great-Aunt Belle had left me a minor league baseball team, a yogurt stand, even a bowling alley; anything but a candleshop and the building it was housed in. She'd died in At Wick's End, and some folks thought it creepy that I'd taken over given the circumstances, but they hadn't read the letter my great-aunt had left me. At Wick's End was her baby, and she'd wanted more than anything else in the world for me to watch over it for her. No one had been more surprised than I had been when I took to candlemaking from the very start, not even Eve Pleasants, the woman who had helped Belle and now worked for me.

"Harrison? Is that you?"

From the shadows of one of the storefronts, Heather Bane appeared. In her mid-twenties, Heather ran The New Age, a shop full of crystals and tomes on spiritual healing, situated next door to At Wick's End. Heather's long blonde hair was pulled back into a ponytail, and she was wearing a tie-dyed smock over her blue jeans and T-shirt. Esmeralda, her store cat and my one-time roommate, flicked her tail at me as they approached.

"Guilty as charged," I said. "You're working late tonight."

She grumbled, "My register totals don't match again. I must be losing it, Harrison, this is the third time it's happened this week. I was trying to figure out how I'd goofed up this time when the lights went off. What's going on with the power?"

I knew the grapevine at River's Edge would spread the news of Aaron's demise soon enough, but I didn't want to be the one to start the story. Still, Heather had a right to know what was happening in one of the shops around us.

"It's Aaron," I said.

Heather's gaze shot to the door behind me. "What about him?"

"I don't know how to tell you this. He's dead."

"Dead?" I wasn't sure what reaction I was expecting, but her trying to fight past me to get into The Pot Shot was not one I'd have considered.

"You can't go in there," I said, holding her arms gently in restraint. "There's nothing we can do. I've already called the sheriff. He's on his way."

"He can't be dead," she started to sob. "He can't be."

"I'm sorry," I said.

She let out a wail that startled Esmeralda, then before I could stop her, Heather shoved her cat into my arms and raced for her car. Oddly, her lime-green Volkswagen Beetle was out in front instead of in its usual spot in back of the building with the rest of the tenants.

I called out, "Hey, where are you going? What about your cat?"

Esme tried to twist out of my arms, but I held fast. If that cat managed to slip out of my grasp, I'd have a nightmare of a time trying to find her. Heather was taking the potter's death much harder than I'd expected. Granted, Aaron's death was a shock, but Heather had instantly fallen apart. I knew that everybody reacted to trauma differently, though. It was just starting to sink in with me that one of my tenants was dead. I was still numb, and that was the only thing that was keeping me going. When it hit me later, as I knew it would, I'd have my own shock to deal with.

Heather didn't reply to my questions as she got into her car and drove off, but I could see the tears streaming down her cheeks as she turned toward me for an instant.

AFTER THE SHERIFF drove up and joined me in front of The Pot Shot, Morton gestured to the cat. "Got an eyewitness there, or is that the culprit?"

"She belongs to Heather."

"So where is she?" the sheriff asked.

"She had to run an errand," I said, not wanting to go into Heather's reaction until I'd had a chance to talk to her about it some more.

"So you're stuck cat-sitting."

I stroked Esme's head. "Let's just say we're hanging out together."

Morton raised one eyebrow, then said, "Whatever. Okay, let's see the body. Can you turn some lights on around here? I know times are tough, but you can afford a little electricity, can't you?"

"The power shorted out and blew a fuse. That's how I found him. Pearly and I were both looking for the cause. As far as I know, he's still upstairs. Do you have a flashlight in your car?"

"Absolutely. Give me one second." As I waited for Morton to grab his flashlight, I was glad to be able to put this in the sheriff's hands, whether it was an accident, or more unlikely, a homicide. I'd been forced to look into my Great-Aunt Belle's murder when Morton hadn't believed that her death had been deliberate, but that had been personal, and I had no doubt the sheriff would be able to handle this particular situation. I didn't have time to help even if he asked, which I was certain he wouldn't be doing. I had my star student and number-one customer, Mrs. Henrietta Jorgenson, coming in tomorrow, and we were embarking on a new way to make candles. Earlier we'd learned, with me barely one step ahead of her, rolling candles out of sheets of wax and the basics of pouring hot, melted wax into molds. I was going to teach her the dipping method, and some of its variations, and I'd been practicing like a madman when she'd announced she was ready to tackle a new way to make candles during her last visit. Mrs. Jorgenson had very deep pockets and an honest love for my craft, two things that endeared her to me.

When the sheriff returned with a heavy-duty flashlight that no doubt doubled as a nightstick, I unlocked the door to The Pot Shot and stepped aside so he could enter. It was only natural that Esmeralda and I follow him inside.

"You're not bringing that cat in here, are you?" the sheriff asked.

"Don't worry, I've got her."

He shook his head, but he didn't forbid it, so I figured it was okay. Despite my impromptu earlier pronouncement, the sheriff knelt down and tried to find a pulse. As he searched for the faintest sign of life, there was nothing I could do but watch and wait. I found myself holding my breath as Morton loomed over the dead man. Had I missed something? Was there a chance Aaron hadn't been dead when I'd come in? If so, I'd wasted precious time by not calling an ambulance first.

Morton's attention left the body, then his beam of light trailed across the floor. It appeared to me that the potter had been sitting at his wheel and had crashed onto the floor beside it. Aaron had been about my age, somewhere in his thirties, but I'd already lost one childhood friend to a heart attack, so I knew that was a distinct possibility here. As the sheriff examined the cord that ran from the pottery wheel to the outlet, I said, "He is dead, isn't he?"

"Oh yes, I agree with your diagnosis, Doctor."

"For how long? Can you tell?"

Morton brushed away my questions as if they were circling gnats. "What? I don't know, but it's been a while. Listen, why don't you wait upstairs? I'll find you when I'm finished here."

"Fine by me," I said as I started out with Esme. The cat was quiet in my grasp, almost nestling inward toward me. Could she sense the presence of death in the room, or was it due more to Heather's abrupt abandonment?

"Wait a second," Morton called out as I neared the door. "This is it. It has to be."

"What did you find?" I asked as I hurried back toward him.

The sheriff shined his light on part of the electrical cord, and I could see that it was so frayed some of the wiring was showing through. Beside it was a puddle of water and a nearly empty bucket. "I'd have to say it was accidental," the sheriff said. "Looks like he must have knocked the bucket over and the water hit the wire."

"Then let's unplug it so I can get the power going," I said. I didn't mean to be callous about the whole thing, but I did have a building without electricity.

"Not so fast," the sheriff said. "I need to get photos of all this first."

"You said yourself it was an accident."

Morton said, "You can wait for me to take some pictures first. Hey, where are you going?"

"Upstairs, like you suggested," I replied. "I've got a half-gallon of cherry-chocolate ice cream in my freezer, and if you're going to take as long as I think you are, it's going to melt by the time I get the power back on. Can I bring you a bowl?"

Morton shook his head, then as I walked off, he added, "Maybe just a little."

I carried Esmeralda upstairs, found some kitty litter from her last visit and used an old pan of Belle's for a litter box. I'd picked up a few extra cans of food at the store for her, just in case she came visiting again. Esme seemed pleased by the prospect of eating, and I wondered if Heather had already fed her. Oh well, one extra meal wouldn't do much harm. After she was settled in, I got the ice cream out and scooped two bowls of it.

By the time I got back downstairs, Morton was nearly finished with his flash photography. Pearly was standing by the doorway watching intently.

The second he saw me, he reached for one of the bowls. "You're a scholar and a gentleman, Harrison Black. Thanks, I can surely use this." He took a bite, then said, "Ice cream is man's finest hour, wouldn't you say?"

"I'd have to go with penicillin, but I like the way you think."

Pearly gestured inside with his spoon. "Terrible business, that."

I nodded, then watched as Morton came out, put his camera down, and took the other bowl out of my hands. Oh well, there was enough for one more serving upstairs, if it didn't melt by the time I got back to it.

The sheriff took a bite, then said, "I pulled the plug from the outlet, so if you want to reset the breaker, you'll most likely have power."

Pearly said, "I'll do it instantly." I was kind of hoping he'd forget about his ice cream, but he remembered and took it with him back to the boiler room where the fuse box stood.

Less than a minute later, half the stores in River's Edge lit up, including At Wick's End, The New Age, and The Pot Shot in front of us. "That will make taking the rest of the photos easier," Morton said. "I'll be here a while, but I'd like to talk to you before I leave. Will you be upstairs?"

"I wish, but no, I'll be in the candleshop. I've got a big day tomorrow, and I've got to get ready for it."

"No rest for the landlord, is there? I'll be by soon."

I made a detour back upstairs before going to the

candleshop. I wanted to check on Esmeralda. I was concerned when I couldn't find her anywhere in the apartment, but when I looked in my small bedroom again, I found her curled up on my pillow, sound asleep.

It appeared that she had settled into my place quite nicely.

I headed back downstairs, jiggling the door to The New Age as I walked past. At least Heather had locked up before coming to find me in front of the pottery shop. I had assumed she had been outside looking for me after the power outage, but after seeing her reaction when I'd told her of Aaron's death, I suddenly wasn't all that sure.

As I reentered At Wick's End, I tried to put Aaron, Heather, and the rest of it all from my mind. Making candles, especially when working with scalding hot wax, is serious business, and I needed every bit of concentration I could give it if I wanted to keep from getting burned.

I WAS BUILDING up a nice blue taper when Morton walked into the store, the chime announcing his arrival. "You're really burning it at both ends, aren't you?"

I tried to smile. "What better place for that than a candleshop? Are you finished?"

"They just took the body away, and I've finished my preliminary work. I've got a forensic team coming in the morning, but with so many folks out sick, it might be a while. I taped the door, just in case, so don't let anyone in there, okay?"

"They won't get in with our key," I said, "But I can't stand around and guard the place."

"You've got your hands full, don't you," he said as he gestured to the wax.

"You want to know the truth? It's great fun. I'd be happy to give you a lesson sometime, if you're interested."

Morton shook his head. "Thanks, but I think I'll pass."

"You don't know what you're missing," I said.

He looked around, then said, "I've got a pretty good idea. Oh, that's right. You don't know about my ex-wife. She was quite the candlemaker. The whole thing kind of left a bad taste in my mouth, you know?"

"Well, if you ever change your mind, I'm here," I said.

Morton tipped his hat, then left me to my dipping.

I glanced at the clock and saw it was approaching ten. If I was going to be fresh in the morning for my one-on-one class, I needed to get some rest. Besides, there wasn't all that much wax left floating on top of the water, and what was there was starting to congeal.

I still probably had time for that last bowl of ice cream before I went to sleep.

SOMETIME IN THE middle of the night, I bolted upright in bed in pitch darkness, having barely survived a dream where I was attacked by a giant feather duster that was trying to choke me.

Esme barely stirred on the pillow beside me as her tail flopped lazily toward where my face had just been.

It was going to take some time getting used to sleeping with a cat in my bed, and I wondered when Heather would come back for her charge.

I worried about my new friend, but there was nothing I could do for her at the moment.

And in a few hours, I was going to have to get up and prepare for another assault by Mrs. Jorgenson.

Two

I had half-expected Heather to wake me sometime in the night to collect Esme, but when my alarm clock suddenly jumped to life the next morning blaring out a song I hadn't heard in twenty years, my houseguest was still with me.

"Morning," I said automatically to the cat as I got up and stretched. Esmeralda opened one eye, looked at me as if I'd just handed her a bill for her night's stay, then promptly went back to sleep. What a tough life.

The shower managed to wake me up, but not before I turned off the hot water supply and endured a sudden and heart-stopping icy stream. I'm not normally a proponent of cold showers, but I'd lost too much sleep tossing and turning the night before, and I had to be fresh for Mrs. Jorgenson.

I knew just what would take care of whatever cobwebs remained in my head that the shower hadn't reached. I left fresh water for Esme, added a little food to her bowl, then headed downstairs for a cup of Millie's coffee.

Millie Nelson ran The Crocked Pot, River's Edge's

answer to Starbucks, and she was also quickly becoming my best friend.

"Look what the cat dragged in," Millie said cheerfully as I took a seat at her long counter. There was a display of pumpkin doughnuts on hand, something I'd first tasted recently but had quickly found addicting. As I started to reach for one, she said, "If you can wait two minutes, I'll have a fresh batch ready."

"I can wait. Coffee," I grunted, and Millie laughed.

"Harrison Black, did you tie one on last night?" She was too cheerful to have heard about Aaron Gaston, and I dreaded having to break the news to her.

"You haven't heard," I said as I took a grateful sip of the coffee. It was hot enough to scald, but I barely noticed. The older I get, the harder it is for me to deal with sleep deprivation. And for me, anything short of eight hours is just not enough.

"Heard what?" she asked as two golden pumpkin doughnuts suddenly appear before me.

"Aaron Gaston. He died in his shop last night."

Millie dropped the mug she was holding, and it shattered on the hardwood floor.

"Millie? Are you all right?"

She nodded. "Heather doesn't know yet, does she?"

"She found out last night. The second I told her, she tore out of here like River's Edge was on fire. She even left Esmeralda with me. What's going on?"

Millie ignored my question and retrieved a dustpan and broom from the kitchen. As she swept up the shards of pottery, I asked again. "Why did Heather react like she did?"

"I'm not one to spread idle stories," she said, chasing the last fragment with her broom.

"There's nothing idle about this. A man died here last night."

Millie blanched slightly, then asked, "How did it happen?"

"I'll answer your question if you answer mine," I said.

"You first," Millie insisted.

I nodded. "It was an accident. It appears that a bucket of water spilled on a frayed power cord while he was working."

Millie looked somehow relieved by the news. "Okay then. Heather and Aaron used to go out together."

"How long ago was this?" I couldn't imagine Heather and Aaron together. She'd treated him with frost the few times they'd bumped into each other when I'd been around them both.

"They broke it off just before you came to River's Edge," Millie said evenly. "Evidently it was Aaron's idea. Something about his wife. His ex-wife, I guess I should say."

"Heather must have taken it pretty hard," I said.

"You could say that. Harrison, you should know that Aaron Gaston was a nice enough man most of the time, but he could be a real jerk when it came to his love life. The second his precious ex came back into his life, he dropped Heather in a heartbeat. Of course the reconciliation didn't last, not with that woman's history, but Aaron couldn't even manage to be cordial to Heather after that. It was as if he somehow blamed her for his wife leaving him again."

"Funny, the last time I talked to Aaron, he told me there was a new woman in his life. Then he chuckled and said that he wasn't sure you could call her exactly new. I wonder if it's possible he was talking about his ex-wife? Who knows, he could have even meant Heather."

I took a bite of doughnut, then Millie said, "Are you eating those exclusively, or would you like to branch out a little?"

"What did you have in mind?" I asked. "I'm always open to new things, but you're going to have to go quite a ways to top these."

"The recipe's not quite there yet, but I'm getting close. Maybe you can be my guinea pig tomorrow if I'm ready."

"I'm your man," I said, "But if you keep feeding me like this, I'm going to have start exercising more than just a walk every now and then."

"You can join my health club," Millie said, "Though I confess, all I seem to do lately is pay the monthly fee."

"Thanks, but I think I'll stick with walking for now."

She said, "Then you might want to add an extra lap or two today. This treat isn't exactly low calorie."

"That's my favorite kind," I said as I grabbed my last doughnut, along with the coffee, and headed over to At Wick's End.

Tick Dearborn was opening her antique shop as I walked past, and I thought about moving on to the candleshop, but it appeared I was the designated deliverer of bad news. Tick was a middle-aged woman who'd never grown out of her big-hair phase, and I wondered how much ozone she'd personally destroyed with hairspray every morning in the course of her lifetime. What I liked best about her was that she had a ready smile and always seemed to think the best of people.

"Tick, have you heard the news?"

She turned to me and said, "Were you talking to me, Harrison?"

I saw her eyes were red and she had a handkerchief to her nose. "Never mind. Somebody already told you."

"Told me what?" she said as she dabbed at her eyes. "These allergies are killing me. I'm dripping and stopped up and sneezing my head off. I swear I'm going to move to Arizona."

"Aaron Gaston died last night."

She took a deep breath, then said, "How sad. Was it a car accident? I'm always worried about traveling by automobile."

"No, he died in his shop."

"How tragic. Just like Belle."

I certainly hoped not. I said, "I guess so. Well, I'll let you get back to work."

"Harrison, let me know if there's a service. I think we should all be there."

"I'll do that."

Tick went back to opening her store, Aunt Tick's Antiques. Her real name was Patricia, but she'd told me the story that when her younger sister had been a toddler, she couldn't say that, so she came up with Tick instead of Trish. Tick was in her early fifties and had been selling antiques for the twenty years since her husband had died, leaving her with his inheritance from his own family, an old Victorian mansion stuffed full of antiques.

I felt like a ghoul passing the word around to the folks at River's Edge, but my tenants had a right to know.

After unlocking the door to At Wick's End, I found Eve Pleasants already there, though she wasn't due in for another hour.

"Going for some overtime?" I said with a smile as I locked the door back behind me.

"I wanted to be sure you were ready for this lesson. Harrison, I don't mean to put any extra pressure on you, but we can't afford to lose Mrs. Jorgenson. Not now."

"Are you worried? She seems happy enough."

Eve said, "Let's just keep her that way, shall we?"

I finished up the last bite of my doughnut and said, "There's something I need to tell you. I'm afraid it's bad news."

"Something besides Aaron's death? Is this place cursed, Harrison?"

"How did you hear about it already?" I asked.

Eve looked sheepish for a second, then said, "We live in a small town."

"News travels fast in Micah's Ridge, doesn't it? What did you know about the man? I wasn't around him enough to get much of an impression one way or another."

"He was nice, I suppose, but you should really ask Heather. They were quite close."

"So I've heard." I took a sip of coffee, then asked, "How close were they, would you say?"

Eve started to say something, then obviously changed her mind. "Why don't you ask her? I'm not comfortable discussing this with you." Eve frowned, then added, "Aaron's death is going to leave you without a tenant. Have you thought about that at all?"

"It never occurred to me," I said. "I suppose I'll put an advertisement in the paper or something."

Eve shook her head. "Belle never advertised, and she managed to keep full occupancy here. She even kept a list of tenants on a waiting list. Didn't you find it in her apartment?"

"I never saw it," I admitted, "But I haven't gone through all her papers, either. It can keep."

"You shouldn't tarry on this, Harrison."

I patted her hand gently. "You worry too much. Everything's going to be fine."

I hoped. I never considered the prospect of any of my tenants leaving, certainly not by dying on the premises. Would anyone even want a store where the owner had died on site? That was how I'd inherited my shop, but I wasn't sure just anyone would be willing to do it. What would happen with Aaron's equipment? Was there an executor, or was that something I was going to have to take care of? I'd have to call Gary Cragg, an attorney with an office on the second floor of River's Edge. Knowing Cragg, he'd probably charge me for the advice, but I had to ask someone.

That was all I needed, more details to muddy my mind when I should have been focusing on dipping candles.

* * *

I HAD JUST finished practicing my third dipped candle of
the day when Heather came in.

Eve saw her and said, "I'll go see what she wants, Harrison. Finish your candle."

I studied the slim tapers in my hand. My previous at-
tempts had all been singles, dipped with one strand of cotton
wick dangling down into the melted wax atop a reservoir of
very hot water. This time I'd decided to try a tandem. Both
ends of the wick were dipped into the wax at the same time,
leaving a narrow strip of untouched wick for me to hang on
to. A couple of the dips had come rather close to immersing
my fingertips, and I was beginning to see Eve's point that I
should have been using a wire holder instead of my own precious hands. Knowing Mrs. Jorgenson, though, she wouldn't
sit still for it. The closer she could get to the process, the better she liked it.

Heather came back with Eve close on her heels. "I'm
sorry, Harrison, I know you're busy, but I want to get Esmeralda."

I glanced at my watch. "My lesson's not for another fifteen minutes. We've got plenty of time."

Eve said, "Give her your key, Harrison, she can get the
cat herself."

I brushed off Eve's advice. After all, At Wick's End was
my store, not hers. Besides, Mrs. J hadn't been early for a
lesson yet.

"Don't worry, I'll be right back," I said as I handed her
the dual tapers in my hand.

"I don't want to put you out," Heather said as we walked
outside. I'd thought about putting in a secret entrance I
could use to get me from my store to my apartment di-
rectly upstairs over the store without leaving the building.
I'd been thinking about a pole like the firemen used, but

that wouldn't do me any good getting back up. As it was, we had to go outside, then up to my place.

"You're not putting me out," I said. "I was happy to watch Esme for you. Do you mind telling me what's going on?"

Heather said, "Yes, I do. Harrison, I don't want to go into it, okay?"

"Fine," I said. If she didn't want to tell me, that was her business.

I unlocked my door, and Heather brushed past me to search for her cat. Esme was still on my bed, asleep on my pillow. She didn't even wake up when Heather collected her.

"Thanks," she said as I locked up behind me.

"Any time. Esme's a pretty good houseguest."

Heather merely nodded, and it was all I could do to keep on her heels as she rushed down the stairs. She managed to duck into The New Age before I could say another word. I saw Mrs. Quimby inside and waved. She was a graying lady with a quick smile and a love for cats and minerals, and she helped Heather out now and then with both.

I thought about following Heather into her store and not leaving until she gave me some reason for dumping Esme on me like she had. Millie had said Heather and Aaron had dated, but it had been over before I came to River's Edge. Was her reaction because of unresolved feelings toward the potter, or was there more to it than that?

I glanced at my watch and realized any cross examinations would have to wait. Mrs. Jorgenson was due in five minutes, and I had just enough time to get things ready for her first lesson in dipping candles.

"I TOLD YOU not to go," Eve said shrilly as I walked into the store.

"I've still got five minutes to spare," I said as I walked in.

"You've got more time than you think," she said with a

grim shake of her head. "Mrs. Jorgenson's come and gone. We've lost her, Harrison."

"What do you mean, we've lost her? I had five minutes." I said the last a little harsher than I should have.

Eve said, "She came thirty seconds after you left, walked into the store, looked around in a huff before I could say a word, then stormed out. I was so stunned by her reaction that I didn't even have a chance to apologize."

"She was early," I repeated, hoping if I said it enough times, it would make a difference. "What makes you think she's not coming back?"

Eve said, "I've seen that look before, Harrison. You get only one chance with a woman like Mrs. Jorgenson."

I shrugged. "I'm sorry she's going to be so stiff-necked about it, but I wasn't wrong to leave when I did."

"You've lost our best client because of a cat that doesn't even belong to you. Can't you see this is a loss we'll not easily recover from?"

"Okay, I'll admit Mrs. Jorgenson's cash infusion was nice, but we'll do all right without it."

Eve raised an eyebrow. "Do you honestly believe that, or are you just trying to make yourself feel better about blowing it?"

"A little of both, probably," I said. "There's nothing I can do about it now."

"I suppose you're right. It had to end sooner or later," Eve said.

"It's just too bad it's sooner," I said, trying to scrape up a grin. It was a pretty feeble attempt. I knew how close to the bone things were run around At Wick's End, not to mention River's Edge. With the double blow of losing a tenant and a star student in the same twenty-four-hour period, I was losing some of the glow I'd had earlier myself.

* * *

AS FATE WOULD have it, Eve and I endured the slowest day we'd had since I'd come to At Wick's End. One older man came in asking for directions and I sold one of our smallest packages of wicks to another customer. I didn't even cover the day's electricity bill by the time Eve's shift was over.

As she was leaving, she said, "Well, that was a day to forget."

"At least the deposit slip will be easy to make out. On second thought, maybe I'll skip a day."

"If you do, Ann Marie will have a fit. She'll think you forgot."

Ann Marie Hart was our bookkeeper, and she watched over the store as if it were her own. "Okay, you've convinced me. See you tomorrow."

"I'll be here, whether any of our customers show up or not." On that cheerful note she left.

I thought about closing the store, since the day was turning out to be a wash. Eve didn't work every hour I did, but then again, she didn't own At Wick's End. That also meant I could close whenever I wanted to, and I was tempted. Still, the hours on the door said OPEN TILL 9, so I thought I'd at least give it another hour or two and see what might happen. I might even make that electric bill.

AFTER AN HOUR, I'd had enough. I was just scrawling out a sign that said, OPEN TOMORROW 9 A.M., when someone came in. "May I help you?" I asked as a tall stranger with the thinnest face I'd ever seen in my life came in.

"Markum," he said in high-pitched voice.

"Upstairs. Third door on your left."

He looked around the room, then backed out slowly. Markum was River's Edge's own salvage expert, whatever that meant. I liked the fellow, big and robust with a ready laugh, but I still couldn't help wondering what exactly it was that he did. As he'd told me once, salvage could cover a great many things.

It was a hopeless day for sales. I taped my homemade sign to the door and slid the deadbolt in place so I could run the register tape and call it a night. I wasn't three steps from the door when someone pounded on it. Markum's visitor probably couldn't find the staircase.

I opened the door and found a frazzled woman with wisps of hair falling down around her face. There was flour on her blouse and something that looked a lot like Silly Putty clinging tenaciously to one shoe. The look of desperation on her face had been enough to make me open the door.

"Thank you, thank you," she said as she rushed in past me.

"Is there something in particular I can help you with?" I asked.

"I'm having a party for my daughter. She's ten years old today. I ran out of games," she added, nearly out of breath. "Do you have anything twenty-four girls can do? Please, you've got to help me."

"I've got just the thing," I said as I led her back to the packets of sheet wax and wicks. "Sheet candles are easy to roll, and it can keep them busy if you have cookie cutters, too."

"Show me," she said.

I tore open a pack, snipped off some wick, then rolled a candle out of a sheet of golden beeswax.

She said, "It's too quick."

"That's where the cookie cutters come in." I grabbed one, cut out four stars and built another candle.

She nodded. "I'll take fifty packs," she said, shoving her credit card in my face.

"I'll give you a quantity discount for that."

After I rang up the sale, I grabbed packets from the storeroom, pulling a rainbow of colors for her, and carried the box out to her car. As I slid the packets onto the front seat, I asked, "Who's watching them now?"

"My husband. I wanted to take them to the movies, but he said it was too expensive, that we should have a nice little party at home. When I left he was ready to hand them all twenties and drop them off at the mall." A soft smile crept to her lips as she added, "I think I'll take the long way home. Twenty more minutes ought to do it."

I waved good-bye as she drove off at a rather sedate pace, then locked the store up yet again. At least I'd managed to cover a few of the utilities with the final sale. The entire day's receipts hadn't come close to touching what I'd lost when Mrs. Jorgenson had walked out on me. Should I call her and apologize? Blast it all, no. I hadn't done anything wrong, and while my customer service skills had come a long way since I'd taken over At Wick's End, I wasn't about to say I was sorry for not being more than five minutes early for a candlemaking lesson.

We'd just have to find a way to limp along without Mrs. J's cash influx.

I wasn't in the mood to run a report from the cash register, and though my bookkeeper would no doubt scold me about it, there wasn't anything that needed doing that couldn't wait.

I put the money from the till in our safe, turned out the lights, and locked up.

What I needed was a hot shower, a bite to eat, and a good book. I'd read through my late Great-Aunt Belle's Agatha Christie books and had moved on to her Charlotte MacLeod collection.

I nearly missed the blinking light on my answering machine upstairs, and I debated ignoring it, but there was something about not knowing who was on the other end that wouldn't give me a moment's peace until I hit the play button.

After I had, I found myself wishing I'd ignored it.

Three

I punched the button and heard Ann Marie Hart's voice, and from the sound of it, my accountant was not happy. "I just heard about Aaron. You need to fill that slot fast, Harrison. Call me."

I couldn't face any more talk of my imminent doom, so I decided Ann Marie could wait till morning. Why hadn't she called the store instead of my apartment, anyway? My place upstairs was the only sanctuary I had.

Well, that wasn't entirely true. I had Belle's little hideaway roof terrace, and tonight would be the perfect time to get away from the world.

I grabbed an old rugby jersey, made a quick sandwich, and collected a Coke from the fridge, then balanced it all as I climbed up the rungs in my closet to the roof. The air was starting to bite as I threw back the hatch, and I was glad I'd brought the jersey with me. I put the scuttle access back down and plugged a cord into an outlet nearby. Suddenly a twinkling lane of white icicle lights lit my way. I'd made a few improvements since taking over River's Edge, but none as important to me as the work I'd done on my get-away from the world. I pulled my folding recliner chair out of a waterproof storage bin I'd hauled up the stairs and set it up under the stars. The jersey, as warm as it was, couldn't hold back the chill of the wind coming off the Gunpowder River, so I retrieved one of Belle's whimsical blankets, this one sporting ice-skating penguins, and wrapped it around me before I sat down. The stars were glorious, and I was glad again that River's Edge was far enough away from town to give me such a view. I ate my sandwich and drank my soda, taking in the smells of autumn as the breeze kicked up, catching hints of wood smoke in the air. Belle's apartment had a tiny woodstove in one corner, and I'd been waiting for a chance to fire it up. It looked like tonight was the night.

But not just yet. On the river below me, I heard a boat go by, wondering what kind of lunatic would be out on the water, as chilly and as dark as it was. Then I had to laugh. It was probably the same kind of idiot up on a roof all by himself at night. A lot had happened in my life lately, and I missed not having someone special to share it with, but I'd learned that love wasn't something I could make happen. Until it came along again, I'd have to be content with what I had, which was a very full life with people I cared about.

I stayed as long as I could stand the chill wind, then reluctantly put my blanket and chair away, gathered up my trash, and headed back downstairs.

I'd laid a fire in the stove two weeks before, just waiting for the first opportunity to use it. The pinecones I used as kindling jumped to life, and in no time at all I had a blaze going. I knew it wasn't all that energy efficient to leave the stove door open, but I loved to see the flames dance, to hear the popping embers, and smell that smoky aroma.

I decided to take an extended hot shower before I settled in, and after a nice long steam, I was fully relaxed. I grabbed *A Pint of Murder* and dove into it, glad for the opportunity to visit another world.

The pounding on my door took me out of the missive as surely as if someone had snatched the book from my fingertips.

"Good. You're still awake," Markum said as he brushed past me into the apartment. His black hair, wild and untamed as always, was in dire need of a haircut, and his chin sprouted the beginnings of a full, dark beard.

"I know I don't keep your hours, but it's barely ten, I'm still up," I said. "Getting ready for winter?" I added as I gestured to his chin.

Markum rubbed it with a huge hand and said, "Going to Alaska next month, so I thought I'd get a little extra insulation."

"What takes you so far away?" I asked.

He shrugged. "A chance at salvage. Say, want to join me? I could use an extra hand. The pay's good, and I can promise you an adventure you'll not soon forget."

I said, "I've got a shop to run, and all of River's Edge along with it. Thanks for asking though." A part of me believed that going along with Markum would be exactly the adventure he promised, and I'd been hoping to get a look at just what his salvaging entailed, but the wiser part of me decided being at River's Edge was adventure enough. Still, maybe someday I'd surprise us both and take him up on his offer.

Markum said, "Heard about Gaston. Accidents can kill you just as dead as the bad guys can."

"Did you know him?" I asked, surprised that Markum's path would cross the potter's at all.

"The man liked working nights as much as I do. Every so often we'd share a sip of whiskey and tell a few lies. He deserved better than he got. I heard you're the one who found him. How did he die?"

"Sheriff Morton says he must have kicked over a bucket of water and shorted out his pottery wheel. The cord was frayed, I saw that myself."

Markum said intently, "You say he was at an electric wheel?"

"That's where we found him."

A cloud crossed Markum's face. "I don't believe it."

"What is it?"

"Gaston hated electric wheels. Ask anybody in his crowd, he was a stickler for the old ways, and that included using a kick wheel."

"I don't mean to show my ignorance," I said, "but what exactly is a kick wheel?"

"It's human powered, there's not a motor on it. Gaston claimed it was the only way he could get the feel for the clay he was throwing. You need to let Morton know that."

"Why don't you tell him yourself?" The last thing I wanted to do was to get embroiled in another murder investigation.

"The sheriff and I don't exactly see eye to eye," Markum admitted. "There was an incident in our past that was open to interpretation; he chose to see things his way, and I chose another. Since then I've done my best to avoid him. But you need to tell him, Harrison. He can't let this go down as an accident, not like that. Will you tell him?"

I said reluctantly, "I guess so, but he's going to want to know why I didn't tell him before."

Markum tapped his nose. "Tell him you heard it through the grapevine here, he'll believe that quick enough." Markum glanced at his watch, then said, "It's late, I need to go."

"I thought you stayed up most of the night," I said.

"It's not time for bed, I've got a call to make. Call him, Harrison."

I agreed, and Markum left the apartment to talk to worlds unknown to me. Should I call the sheriff now, or wait until morning? Who was I kidding? There was no way I'd get any reading done until I made the call. With any luck he'd be out and I could leave a message. I was in no mood to talk to the sheriff myself.

Wouldn't you know it, he picked up on the first ring.

"Morton here."

"Sheriff, I heard a rumor that puts some doubt on your theory about Aaron Gaston's death being accidental."

"What have you heard?" he asked without trying to hide the irritation in his voice.

"He used only a kick wheel, never an electric one."

"What's the difference, Harrison?"

"One runs on electricity, one works with a kicking foot. There's no motor on the wheel he used."

Morton chewed on that a second or two, then said, "Maybe he was playing around with it and got burned."

"That's not the way I heard it," I said.

"Then why did he have one if he didn't use it? Answer me that."

I thought about it a second, then said, "It must have been there for his students. He teaches . . . taught classes just like I do. I'm sure it was there for his students."

"You don't know that, you're just guessing, aren't you?"

I said, "What would it hurt to ask someone who knew him better than either one of us?"

Morton asked, "Do you have anyone in particular in mind?"

There was no way I was going to give him Heather's name, not with the way she was acting lately. Then I remembered the ex-wife. "Isn't his ex a potter? If anybody should know, she should. Why don't you call her?"

"If I do, will it get you off my back?"

"I just thought you should know," I said.

He took so long to answer I nearly gave up on him when Morton added, "Okay, I'll look into it. And Harrison . . ."

"Yes," I said.

"Thanks for calling."

I was so shocked by his thanks that I couldn't think of anything to say before he hung up. I stoked the fire, added another small piece of wood, then went back to my book. My hand automatically went down to my lap where Esmeralda liked to sit when I read, and I wondered briefly if I should get a cat myself. I'd never felt all that alone living by myself before, but the apartment, as small as it was, was starting to feel too big for just one person. No, I'd get used to it, just as I'd gotten used to everything else that had come my way. I was just beginning to think of my living quarters as my apartment and not Belle's. With a little time, I was certain I'd be fine without a roommate of any kind.

Even a feline one who tended to hog the pillows at night.

MY BOOKKEEPER, ANN Marie, was waiting for me at Millie's the next morning when I stopped in before opening the candleshop. "There you are," she said.

"I didn't realize we had a breakfast appointment," I said with a smile as I grabbed a blueberry muffin instead of pumpkin as a change of pace. Millie handed me a coffee, then said, "Are you going to be around later?"

"I'll be at the shop all day. What's up?" Then I remembered our earlier conversation. "Did you nail your new recipe?"

"You'll see," she said, adding a quick smile.

I joined Ann Marie at her table. "Now what's so urgent? I know I have a storefront vacant, but there's nothing I can do about that right now."

She tapped a pencil against the tabletop, beating out a staccato accompaniment to her words. "The building has to run at full occupancy, especially on the first floor. You need every dime you've got coming in to stay afloat."

"I know that, Eve's been after me too, but isn't The Pot Shot paid up until the end of the month?"

Ann Marie shook her head. "You'd think so, wouldn't you? Unfortunately, your late Great-Aunt Belle liked to do things a little differently. She staggered the rents so that she had at least some income every week. I told her it was an accounting nightmare, but Belle liked to get money more than once a month. She said it made it feel like Christmas."

"I don't even have to ask when Aaron's rent was due, do I?"

Ann Marie paused the beat of her pencil. "It was due yesterday. You need to jump on this, Harrison."

"Fine," I said, focusing on my breakfast instead of my worries. It was too late. Not even Millie's fine baking could pep me up after Ann Marie's pronouncement. I didn't have much time at all before things started to fall down around my ears, according to everyone around me.

Ann Marie had to notice my suddenly slumped shoulders. She stopped tapping her pencil altogether and smiled softly at me. "It's not as bad as all that. You've actually got six days to find another tenant before your electric bill is due."

"Wow, six whole days," I said. "Listen, I know you're just trying to help. I'll see if I can round up Belle's list of potential tenants and find out if any of them are still interested. Thanks for dropping by."

She took the hint, swallowing the last of her coffee and waving good-bye to Millie.

I was still staring at my muffin when Millie came by to top off my coffee. "Don't let the monkeys get you down," she said.

I smiled in spite of my gloom. "Where did you come up with that one?"

Millie said, "My Uncle Timothy used to say there were kind people on this earth, and then there were monkeys, folks who never evolved past throwing bananas at each other. It's not the people who try to bring you down, it's the monkeys."

"He sounds like an odd bird," I said.

"And proud of it, truth be told. You should meet him. He's as full of spit and vinegar as anyone I've ever met."

"Next time he's in town, bring him by."

Millie studied me a moment, then said, "Yes, I believe you would get along just fine with my uncle. Now don't you have a candleshop to run?"

I glanced at my watch. "No private lessons today, so I'm not in any rush."

Millie said, "Well I am, I can't stand around here all day and listen to you." She softened her words with a flick of her towel. "I've got baking to do."

"Don't forget, I want to be one of your tasters."

"Oh you're on my list, all right. Now shoo."

I walked out of The Crocked Pot as Tick walked in.

"Morning, Harrison. It's a stunning day, isn't it?"

"You're feeling better, aren't you?"

"I found a wonderful new allergist. I believe he's cured me."

"That's excellent news," I said. After Tick went inside, I took a deep breath of the cool autumn air. It was my favorite time of year, bar none, and I wished, for just a moment, to have the leisure to enjoy it more instead of spending the day inside At Wick's End. I'd always thought being my own boss would give me freedom from punching clocks and nosy supervisors. Instead, I found that I worked harder for myself than I ever had for any employer. I was, without a doubt, the toughest boss I'd ever dealt with. Well, there had to be perks to running my own show. Eve was slated to work the evening shift, and I'd always worked alongside her. Not tonight. Come 4:00 P.M., I was going to take the rest of the day off.

I peered in Heather's new age shop as I walked past it,

wondering if she'd come to grips yet with losing an old love. Since my parents had died in a car wreck on my twenty-first birthday, I hadn't lost a soul I was close to until my Great-Aunt Belle was murdered.

To appease my conscience for cutting out early, I decided to open At Wick's End half an hour early. Eve came in three minutes after I flipped the sign to OPEN.

"You must have hit it by accident," she said as she flipped it back.

"No, I thought I'd get a jump on things," I said as I set it back.

"We never opened early," Eve said with a snort. "Belle always said if we did, soon enough folks would expect it every day."

"Well, I don't think one day is going to start any bad trends, one way or another. Chances are nobody's going to show up early anyway. I just felt like opening. Eve, did you ever used to work the store by yourself, or was Belle here every second the store was open?"

"Goodness no, she took a day off now and then. She said she had to or she'd go stir crazy."

"I'm getting a little antsy myself," I admitted. "I haven't missed a minute of work since I took over, and it's starting to get to me. I'm thinking about cutting out at four, if you wouldn't mind."

"Mind? Why should I mind, Harrison? It's your shop, after all. I'll be fine on my own."

She sounded almost eager to get me out of there, but I wasn't going to push it. Eve could probably use the space as much as I could. Though she'd been a godsend teaching me about candles, I was certain she longed for a little quiet time at work just waiting on customers and not educating her new boss.

* * *

I **WAS JUST** getting ready to grab some lunch when Mrs. Jorgenson walked into At Wick's End.

"Good morning," she said brusquely. "I assume you're ready for me."

I nodded, too surprised to say a word. So she'd come back after all. Eve started to greet her, caught one look at the expression on her face and stepped back into the storeroom where she'd been preparing an order.

I'd never gotten around to cleaning up from the day before, so the table looked as if I'd set it out fresh just for her. Before I could say a word, Mrs. Jorgenson said, "I must apologize for my behavior yesterday. I didn't realize until I arrived at the store that our lesson wasn't until today. I must have written it down wrong in my book. I've been doing that more and more lately. Too much on my mind, I suppose."

"No harm done," I said, ready to accept her fabrication if it meant keeping her coming back. "So, are you ready to get started learning a new technique today?"

"I'm quite excited, actually," she said. "How do we begin?"

I got out an old shoebox and handed her a hammer and screwdriver, along with a hefty block of translucent wax. She asked, "What happened to the plastic bags?"

"This system works a lot better," I said. I'd stumbled across it in one of my books and had found it to be much more effective than using a plastic bag to break up the wax in. "Chisel off small chunks," I ordered as I went over my supplies again. Mrs. J took the safety glasses and slid them into place, then attacked the wax with glee. She was enjoying it a little too much, and I realized she was getting out a lot of aggression. Good for her; it was the cheapest therapy I'd ever heard of.

When she had enough wax chipped off the main body, I stopped her, but not until she'd given it a few extra wacks. I pulled out what remained of the block and broke up a few of the larger chunks, then slid the fragments into the double boiler. As the wax started to melt, I asked, "Would you like to add color and fragrance, or will we be making the economy model today?"

"Harrison, you know I always start with the basics. What do we do next?"

I measured out some wick and said, "The first few times it might be better to do single tapers, just until you get the hang of it." I'd laid out some of my earlier efforts and showed her what I'd done. She picked up a few of the singles, then examined a double I'd done in beeswax. I could tell she wanted to jump a few steps, something I would have been delighted to do, but her analytical approach held fast as she put the candles back on the tabletop.

"Where do we begin?"

I peered inside the double boiler, then said, "It looks good. Let's get started."

"Shouldn't we check the temperature first?"

I looked at the pool of melted wax. It looked exactly like water, and the first time I'd done it I thought my double boiler must have been leaking. "It looks just right to me."

I took a pot of boiling water off another burner and poured it into a stainless steel cylinder I used as a dipping can.

"You put water in there first?" she asked, incredulous.

"Absolutely. Now we add the wax." I gently eased the melted wax into the container, with Mrs. Jorgenson close enough to breathe my air. After close examination, she said, "I can't see a difference. Did it all mix together?"

"Look at the sides of the container. You can see the line where the wax ends and the water begins. When you use dye in the wax, it's really easy to see."

I handed her a piece of number-one wick and said, "Dip away. Just remember, use quick, even dips, then give the wax a chance to cool between immersions, and you'll have a candle in no time."

By the tenth dip, she barely had any wax on her wick at all. "How long does this process take?"

It had never taken me more than three or four dips to get some kind of buildup on the wick. Something had gone wrong. I thought about all I'd read, then realized the wax was probably too hot.

"Tell you what," I said matter-of-factly, "Let's allow it to cool a little first."

"The wax on my wick, or what's in there?"

"Both," I said.

We waited a few minutes and I decided to test it with a piece of wick of my own. After three dips, along with a little waiting time between immersions for cooling, I had the beginnings of a taper.

"Now why can't I do that?" Mrs. Jorgenson asked impatiently.

"It's all yours," I said.

After a few minutes, she had a thin taper herself, one of frosty white wax. "Why, it looks just like a miniature icicle." The delight in her voice was impossible to miss.

"You're a natural," I said as she continued to dip. Before too long, she had a fine, stout taper and announced that it was complete. Before I could say a word, she said, "I'd like to do another."

I looked into the container and saw that we had plenty of wax left. She took the offered wick and began dipping it immediately. After Mrs. Jorgenson was into making her fourth candle, she said, "What's wrong with the wax now?"

I looked and saw that there was a skim coat of wax forming on top. "It's supposed to do that. It's starting to cool."

She nodded, but continued to dip.

I said, "You really should stop now. It's not fit for dipping."

"Nonsense. I want to experiment." As the wax began to congeal, she picked up lumps of it onto her candle. The shape was exotic and not altogether unattractive. "There, it's perfect," she announced, and I had to admit she'd been right.

"Do I have to let these cool overnight?" she said, eyeing her creations with joy.

"No, ma'am, as soon as they cool to the touch, they're ready to go. Give them another ten or fifteen minutes and they'll be set."

"Excellent," she said. "That will give me time to gather my supplies. Aren't you coming?"

"I'm right behind you," I said, happy that she'd come back for reasons more than her money. In Mrs. Jorgenson I had a true kindred spirit in wax. On the surface, we had nothing in common. She was a rich, older widow with time on her hands, and I was a fairly young man doing everything I could to keep my head above water. But when we were working on candles, we were two of a kind.

After picking out our nicest double broiler and dipping can, Mrs. J added more wax to her substantial collection, along with a thick roll of wick and a wide variety of colors and scents. "I can't wait for our next lesson. Do you have anything special in mind?"

"There are a lot of things we can do with dipping candles," I said. "Next week we'll experiment."

She signed the substantial receipt and was humming gladly as she walked out of the store.

"Miracles really do happen," Eve said after Mrs. Jorgenson was gone. "I never believed she would come back."

"I'd like to say it was my charm, but she said she thought she'd written down the wrong day for our lesson."

Eve snorted. "Don't you believe that for one second. She's too sharp to do that. No, I'm guessing that little story was her way to save face. She's got the candle bug, and she's got it bad, Harrison."

"I can't blame her, I've got it myself." Suddenly I didn't feel guilty about taking the evening off anymore at all. "Tell you what, as soon as you get back from lunch, I'm going to call it a day."

Eve nodded. "I think that's a splendid idea. I shan't be long."

She was as good as her word, back in nineteen minutes from the beginning of her hour break. When I tried to protest that she had more time, Eve shooed me out of my own store. "Go now, there's a whole world out there, in case you've forgotten it."

With a sheepish grin, I headed out of At Wick's End with a free afternoon and a little money in my pocket.

It should have been perfect, and it would have been, if I hadn't run into my worst nightmare in the parking lot behind River's Edge before I had a chance to get away.

Four

I tried to duck when I saw Manfred Stratton standing by my truck, but it was too late. He spotted me before I could get back out of sight, and hailed me in his booming voice.

"Harrison. I was just ready to come looking for you. We have a great many things to talk about."

Manfred Stratton had stumbled into At Wick's End two weeks before, and I hadn't been able to shake him since. If the man had shown the slightest interest in candlemaking I might have warmed to him, but instead, he was a former salesman who now had nothing to do but harass shop owners with his windy conversations and pointless stories of his past successes, no doubt many of them accomplished only in his mind.

"Sorry, Manfred, I don't have time to talk." Anyone else would have gotten the hint from the tone in my voice, but Manfred ignored it, as he no doubt had his customers' protestations in the past.

"Fine, fine. I'll buy you a cup of Millie's excellent

coffee and we can visit for a while. Have I ever told you about the time I was nominated for salesman of the year for my company?"

"I'm sure you have," I said as I brushed past him and opened the truck door. "'Bye," I said as I sped away. I'd half-expected Manfred to throw himself in my path to keep me from driving off, but as I turned the corner, I saw that the man was still talking! Remarkable. I wondered how long it would take him to notice that his audience had vanished.

I was learning about all kinds of odd birds that shop owners had to deal with on a daily basis. Manfred, for all his long-winded stories and lack of purchases, wasn't as bad as the shoplifters. It's not like I sold necessities in At Wick's End. What drove some people to steal the wicks and wax I'd caught them with? Eve, having logged much more practice, was a whiz at spotting our light-fingered visitors. The week before she'd collared a sweet, little old man who admitted to pockets stuffed with merchandise.

I drove the thoughts of thieves and windbags from my mind and promised myself I'd have some fun.

Only I wasn't exactly sure what that entailed anymore.

ALMOST BY ACCIDENT, I found myself at the Micah's Ridge pavilion down by the riverfront. There were jewelers and T-shirt shops, small little restaurants tucked into nooks and crannies, and there was a place for open-air concerts that occurred Friday nights throughout the summer. We had two fairs a year, one in summer and the other in autumn, and Eve and I had been discussing a booth rental to test the waters. I parked the truck and walked around the mostly empty grounds until I came to the water's edge. There was a shop there that rented canoes and kayaks that I hadn't seen before. I found a woman in her late twenties out front working on an old wooden canoe.

"Getting your rentals in shape?" I asked as I watched her sand through layers of paint.

She looked up and laughed as she brushed an errant strand of black hair out of her face. "I wouldn't dream of putting this out for rental. This one's going to be all mine."

"So you work at this shop and restore boats, too?"

She smiled. "What can I say? I'm a woman of limited interests." She stuck out a hand and said, "I'm Erin Talbot."

"It's nice to meet you, Erin. My name's Harrison Black."

She nodded, then ran her fingertips across the patch she'd been sanding. As she worked, Erin asked, "Have you ever been out on the water?"

"I canoed at summer camp, but that was a long time ago. Do you get many folks who want to paddle the Gunpowder?" The river was a little too wide and fast for my tastes.

"It's protected here, though how they ever had the nerve to call this Gunpowder Lake I'll never know. I do most of my own serious paddling in the mountains."

"What rivers have you been on?"

"Let's see, I like the Nolichucky, the French Broad, and the Nantahala the best. They're all drivable from here, so I can shut the place down and do it as a day trip." She gestured to her rentals and asked, "Why don't you take one out?"

"A canoe? I don't think so. Unless you'd care to join me. You can even steer."

She laughed. "As tempting an offer as that is, I've got to stay with the shop. If you don't want to canoe by yourself, why don't you try a kayak? I've got some that are lots of fun."

I raised an eyebrow as I said, "Fun is in the eye of the beholder."

"Come on, Harrison, give it a try."

"Why not?" I found myself taking a quick lesson on dry

land, and before I knew what was happening, I was in an open kayak on the water.

"Use the paddle like a windmill," Erin called out to me, and I was amazed to find myself slicing through the water with a great deal more ease than with the remembered canoe. "Hey, this is fun."

"I told you so," she laughed as I sped away.

I was tempted to go all the way up to River's Edge, but I was afraid my muscles would be too sore if I pushed it that hard on my first time out, so I drove myself upstream, then drifted lazily back to Erin's shop. What a sense of freedom being out on the water gave me. I could look down and see fish darting below me one second, then see a wedge of sandbar the next. Where I'd fought with a canoe paddle as a kid, drowning my companion as I switched sides, I took to the kayak instantly. What great fun to glide across the water.

Erin was waiting for me when I slid silently up to her dock. The effect was spoiled somewhat when I failed to stop in time and scraped the side of the kayak on the pier.

"Sorry about that," I said sheepishly as I climbed out.

"These things are designed to take a beating," she said. "Have fun?"

"That was excellent," I said. "I will absolutely be back."

Erin nodded as she settled up my account. "I'll be here. Unless it's a day I head to the mountains."

I walked out of the rental shop, surprised by the stiffness in my shoulders and the tightness on my face. Next time I'd have to use sunscreen before I went out on the water. The only thing I knew for sure was that there would definitely be a next time. Erin intrigued me, and I had to admit that it would be more than the kayak rental that would bring me back to her shop. She was a woman I wanted to get to know better.

It was still too early to head back to River's Edge, so I

decided to stop in at A Slice of Heaven, a pizza place Heather had introduced me to, and grab a bite to eat.

I started for a spot near the jukebox, then saw Heather sitting in the corner by herself. I approached and asked softly, "Care for some company?"

She looked up, startled by the sound of my voice. "Oh. Hi, Harrison."

"Listen, I didn't mean to interrupt, but I'll be over there if you want somebody to talk to."

I started for the place I'd intended to sit all along when she called out, "That's okay, you can stay."

It wasn't the warmest invitation I'd ever gotten in my life, but I sat with her anyway.

I glanced at the menu and said, "What did you order? I'm not sure what I feel like today."

"I don't have much of an appetite," she admitted as she twisted her glass on the table.

"Well, I feel like pizza, and I can't eat one by myself. You don't have to have any, you can take a piece and sneer at it if you want." She wasn't interested in my banter or my smile, but I wasn't going to give up that easily. I saw the owner, April May, wearing an apron that said, "Pizza, the world's most perfect food." Her flaming red hair was pulled back into a braid, and though business was starting to pick up, she trotted right over to our table.

"Hey, Harrison," she offered as she watched Heather carefully. It was clear she was worried about her friend.

"April, may we have a pizza?"

"Gee, I haven't heard that one before," she said with a slight groan. "What can I get for you?"

"We'll take a garb—a Heaven Scent pizza, please. Better make it a medium, Heather said she isn't hungry."

April said, "You know what? I feel like making a large. Hope you don't mind. What you don't eat you can take home for breakfast. Refill, Heather?"

She glanced up at the restaurateur, then back at her soda. "Sure, why not?"

"How about you? What are you drinking?" April asked me.

"I'll have what she's having."

"Two Dr Peppers and a large Heaven Scent. Back in a shake."

"You can stop it now," Heather said as soon as April was out of sight.

"Stop what?"

"Trying to cheer me up. I'm in no mood for it."

I said, "Listen, I'm sorry about what happened to Aaron." The last thing Heather wanted to hear were my suspicions about Aaron's demise.

"It wasn't an accident," Heather said, her gaze on her glass and not on me.

I remembered what Markum had told me and wondered what had brought Heather to the same conclusion. "Why do you say that?"

"Aaron *never* threw his work on an electric wheel," she said. "Somebody should tell the sheriff."

"He already knows," I said, "And he doesn't believe it was foul play for a second. According to Morton, Aaron was experimenting. That's why he never noticed the frayed cord, he wasn't used to working on that wheel."

"That is complete and utter nonsense," Heather said. "You didn't know Aaron all that well, but I can tell you, he was a fanatic when it came to keeping the equipment in his shop in good working order. I'd like to see that cord myself. How badly was it frayed?"

I admitted, "It was pretty bad. But who would want to kill him?"

"Do you mean besides me?" she asked sullenly.

"Come on, you can't believe anyone would think you were a suspect."

Heather started to say something, then stopped when

April came up with our drinks. She noticed the truncated conversation, and for a change April dropped off the sodas and scampered away without comment.

"You were getting ready to say something," I nudged her.

"It's not important. Listen, thanks for trying, but I can't do this."

Before I could stop her, Heather was gone.

I thought about going after her, but when she was finally ready to talk, Heather knew where to find me.

A few minutes later April slid the large pizza in front of me. She said, "Please tell me Heather went to the little girls' room."

"She walked out on me," I said.

"And you didn't stop her?" The cutting tone of her voice raked into me.

"It wasn't up to me. I did what I could."

April studied me a second, then said, "I know it's not your fault. That girl's taking this hard."

"She knows we'll both listen when she's ready to talk," I said. "There's not much else we can do."

"That's the truth. Well, enjoy."

I looked at the pizza, wondering how in the world I was going to make even a dent in it when Erin walked up.

She smiled broadly. "Harrison, are you stalking me?"

"I was just going to ask you the same thing. I was here first, remember? Care to join me?"

"I don't want to intrude. I'll just sit with you until your guest comes back."

I said, "Then you're in for a wait. She just walked out on me."

Erin asked, "What in the world did you say to her?"

"I offered to listen," I said as I took a piece of pizza. "Help yourself."

She took what should have been Heather's plate and served herself a slice. "Thanks, I'm starving."

April came over with another soda and grabbed Heather's

glass. "I see you've made a new friend," she said to me.

We both nodded, then I said, "I started kayaking today. April, this is Erin Talbot."

April looked at Erin and said, "You let him get started on the Gunpowder? You should have had him try the French Broad first. Now that's a kayak ride."

"So you two know each other," I said as I took another bite.

"We're in Micah's Ridge, Harrison, not Charlotte. It's tough not knowing everyone around town."

To my surprise, Erin and I managed to polish off the pizza without any help. When April slipped the bill beside my plate, Erin said, "Let's split that."

"Are you kidding? This is the first date I've been on in six months. Don't spoil it for me."

Erin smiled, took a ten-dollar bill from her purse and slid it across the table. "Sorry to burst your bubble, but this wasn't one either."

"So where would you like to go on our first official date then?"

Erin laughed. "Thanks for asking and all, but no thanks."

"Well, you can't blame a guy for trying," I said.

She got up, then said, "I'll see you later, Harrison."

"My next day off," I promised.

"So you are stalking me," she said.

"No, but I've got a thing for your kayak."

"Let's make sure it just stays at that."

I said, "I can take the hint, Erin. You've already turned me down. If you change your mind and decide you want to go out with me, you're going to have to do the asking yourself."

"Don't sit waiting by the phone," she said.

"What is life without hope?" I said, adding a gentle grin.

"Good-bye, Harrison." She smiled for just a second before she turned to go.

" 'Bye, Erin."

I wasn't sure who had been more surprised by my date invitation, Erin or me. There was something about her, some spark that I liked, that had made me ask, though I hadn't been actively dating since my last breakup. Heather and I had started off with the potential for more, but we were sliding into friendship instead. At least we had been before Aaron Gaston's death. Truthfully, I wasn't sure where we were headed in the long run, since it had been my pattern to date women who had started off as strictly friends.

Erin hadn't been all that pleased when I'd asked her out on a date. My ego wasn't so huge that I couldn't believe she wasn't interested in me. I wasn't sure, and I might have imagined it, but I thought I'd seen some interest in her eyes before I'd asked.

April collected my bill and said, "That's the first time I've ever seen a man lose two women in thirty minutes over one pizza. You should write a book on what not to do with women, Harrison, you'd make a fortune."

I shook my head. "I'm afraid what I know can't be taught. It's a gift you're either born with or you're not."

April said, "Don't beat yourself up over either one of them. Heather's got a lot on her plate at the moment, and Erin's trying to break free from a boatload of bad memories."

"What do you know about her?" I asked, interested in her insight. April seemed to me to be a pretty good judge of character working behind that counter day in and day out.

"If she wants you to know, she'll tell you herself. I wouldn't give up on either one of them, Harrison, those are both jewels in the rough there."

I smiled gently and asked, "Now I know how much the pizza is, but how much should I kick in for the advice?"

She snapped a dishtowel at me and said, "It's a two-for-one special today. The advice is free, worth every penny it cost you."

I nodded. "Thanks. I do appreciate it."

"You're most welcome, not that you'll probably listen to a word of it."

Outside, the sun had slipped away and the darkness was creeping in. The days were getting shorter, and when Daylight Savings Time kicked in soon enough, there would be more night that daytime.

I'd had enough of people for the time being. All I wanted now was to slip quietly into my apartment and spend some time with Ms. MacLeod and my latest mystery.

It turned out that was one more wish I wouldn't be getting that day.

Five

GARY Cragg was waiting at my door when I walked through the hall to my apartment.

"I didn't stand you up, did I?" I asked, knowing full well we hadn't scheduled a meeting, though getting together with the attorney had been on my list of things to do.

"No, but I need to speak with you."

I unlocked my door. "Come on in."

He hesitated outside my apartment, then said, "If you don't mind, I'd rather do this in my office."

It wasn't much of a commute, since his office space was fifty steps from my apartment, but he'd come to see me. Then again, I wasn't a huge fan of Cragg. Did I really want him inside my apartment? It was my refuge, after all.

"Your office it is," I said as I stepped back out and locked my door.

I followed him down the hall and into his office. Cragg took his seat, and I noticed the client's chair across from his desk was lower than a normal chair. It gave the attorney a perfect opportunity to loom over his visitors. The man was always looking for an angle.

"What's so important that it interrupts my time off?" I asked, not even trying to be diplomatic. I knew running River's Edge was a full-time job, but I didn't have to like it.

"Sorry for the late hour, but this couldn't wait." Wow, an apology from a lawyer. I'd have to start keeping a diary just so I could write that one down. He continued, "I need to speak with you about Aaron Gaston's estate."

"He's got an estate? His pottery shop must have done a lot better than my candlemaking business does."

Cragg dismissed my sarcasm and said, "All his worldly goods go to his ex-wife, Sanora Gaston."

"Sounds like he was a generous man. So what do you need me for? She's welcome to come collect his stuff any time."

"That's just it. Ms. Gaston is a potter of no small ability herself. You may not be aware of it, but when River's Edge first opened, she was the co-owner of the business."

"This is all fascinating, but is there a reason you're telling me all this?"

If Cragg was perturbed with my attitude, he was hiding it well. "Ms. Gaston has approached me about the possibility of taking over the shop, including the lease. Aaron's agreement is good until nearly the end of the year, but she's interested in negotiating occupancy for a longer period, say three years."

I'd gone through some of Belle's papers and I knew she never offered more than one year of guaranteed occupancy to any of her tenants, including At Wick's End. "That's out of the question," I said. I wasn't ready to change any of Belle's policies unless I believed there was a sound reason for it. My late great-aunt was a savvy businesswoman, much better at running things than I was, so if I erred, I wanted it to be on the side of caution.

Cragg frowned, steepled his fingers in front of him, then

said, "Am I to understand you are against her occupancy under any conditions?"

"She's not getting a renewal like that," I said. I'd always had a problem with authority figures, and the best way to get me to do something was to tell me I couldn't.

"Very well. She will be satisfied, for the interim, to take on the remaining months of the lease."

Suddenly I was feeling very stubborn. I knew how much I needed a paying tenant, but I felt like I was the unwilling guest on Cragg's little railroad. "Not until I meet her first."

"Harrison, are you trying to be difficult?" the attorney said, his temper breaking through a bit.

"It's my building, and as far as I can tell, it's my right."

Cragg pursed his lips, then reached for the telephone. Before I knew what was happening, I heard him say, "Mr. Black would like to meet you. Now. As soon as you can get to my office."

"You didn't call her, did you?" I asked.

"Isn't that what you just demanded, Harrison?"

I stood up. "Not tonight. It's too late for a meeting, and I'm tired."

"But I've already called her."

"Then you can call her back and tell her to come by At Wick's End in the morning."

I started for Cragg's door when it opened. A pretty, young blonde came in wearing faded jeans and a red top.

I started to go past her when she stuck out a hand. "Hi, I'm Sanora."

"That was quick," I said.

"I was outside on the steps enjoying the night. I always loved being here when everyone else was gone. I used to sit on the steps outside and watch the river go by."

Cragg said, "I'm sorry to have bothered you, but it seems Mr. Black wants to postpone your meeting until tomorrow."

I started to protest when Sanora said, "That's fine. I know we kind of surprised you with all this. The more I thought about coming back to River's Edge, the more sense it made. Gary was nice enough to agree to talk to you about it, but I should have come to you myself. I'll see you tomorrow."

"Wait a second," I said. "Since you're already here, I don't suppose it will hurt to talk about it."

She considered it for a moment, then said, "Only if you're certain. I don't want to take up your free evening. I know how valuable those can be."

"It's not a problem." I looked over at Cragg and saw he was hanging on every word she spoke. Did he have a thing for Sanora? He was definitely showing more than an expected interest in her coming back to River's Edge. In all the time I'd owned the place, it was only the second time I'd ever seen the attorney hanging around after his regular business hours.

For spite, I added, "Why don't we go down to the pottery shop? We can talk about it there. Thanks, Gary," I said, stressing his first name as Sanora had.

"Glad to help. Why don't I join you? I'm finished here."

Sanora said, "I'm sure we'll be fine. Thanks again."

Out in the hallway, I said, "Just let me grab the key for The Pot Shot first."

She started to say something, but then thought better of it. I found the key Pearly had given me, then followed Sanora downstairs.

I was afraid going back into the pottery store might be a little traumatic for her, and she was indeed quiet as I unlocked the door. I asked, "Would you rather do this tomorrow morning? I know this can't be easy on you."

She shook her head. "Aaron and I made our peace before he passed away. We were friends at last. You can't believe how much comfort I've taken from that." She put a hand on my arm as she added, "In all honesty, we were actually better friends than we were a couple."

"Won't it be hard for you working here, knowing what happened to him?"

She frowned gently. "I thought about that, believe me, but we built this place together. What more fitting tribute could there be than continue it? I'm sure Aaron would have wanted it that way. I do hope you'll give me that lease. Three years will make this place feel like home."

I started to agree, then realized what I'd told Cragg. I'd already committed myself. "I'm afraid that's not going to happen, at least not for now. Why don't you finish out Aaron's lease, it runs through November. We can talk about extensions then."

"If that's what you want," she said. "Was it . . . here that it happened?"

She gently touched the wheel Aaron had been working at, as if afraid it would bite her.

"Yes. Some of the folks around here think it was odd that he was throwing on an electric wheel."

"Aaron was always trying something new. It wouldn't surprise me at all that he was throwing on it, goodness knows I nagged him enough to try it. I prefer electric, myself. When I used a kick wheel, my legs ached at the end of the day." She dusted her hands off, as if removing the last remnant of the wheel's touch, then said, "So I can move in?"

I nodded. "I hate to bring this up, but the rent is due for the business. Actually, it's a few days late."

She nodded. "Then let's take care of that right now. I'm sure Gary is still upstairs, and I've got my checkbook."

I agreed. It would be best to just go ahead and get it all out of the way. I looked at it as one less thing to worry about. Then perhaps Eve and Ann Marie would stop nagging me.

We signed the papers creating a new lease for Sanora, covering just the short term until Aaron's year was up. Even if she didn't work out as a tenant, I'd bought myself two more months of rent, and a little breathing room.

What an adventurous afternoon off I'd had. My shoulders were stiffening up from my kayaking experience and the slight sunburn I'd gotten was getting redder by the moment. A hot shower took most of the ache out of the burn, but by the time I was finished, I barely had enough energy to keep my eyes open. I'd read just two pages of my book when it dropped to my chest, and I fell fast asleep.

FROM THE BEATING my front door was taking, someone was trying to break into my apartment. At least that's what it sounded like when I woke up the next morning. I stared at the alarm clock through bleary eyes and saw that it was just a little past six A.M.

Grabbing a robe on my way out of the bedroom, I opened the door to find Heather Bane glaring at me, madder than a wet cat.

She started in on me before I could open my mouth. "Harrison Black, of all the no-brain, thickheaded, idiotic things to do, I can't believe you did it."

"What was I supposed to have done?" I asked, trying my best to wake up. I was no match for Heather, certainly not still half-asleep, though I was coming around pretty quickly under the tirade.

"You let that woman back into our lives."

"What woman? Erin?" Now what was she talking about?

"Sanora, you nit! I can't believe she's here. You've got to throw her out, Harrison. Tear up the check, give her a refund, I don't care what it takes, but she's got to go."

"Take it easy, Heather. I don't know what all the fuss is about. She said she was a tenant here with Aaron from the very start."

"Before me, is that what you're saying? Did you happen to ask her why she left?"

"I assumed it was because of the divorce," I said. "Listen, can we discuss this over a cup of coffee?"

"I've had mine, thank you very much. You assumed wrong. Belle threw her out. She told Aaron that either Sanora went alone, or they both did. What do you think about that?"

"It's hard for me to believe Belle would do something like that. What happened?"

Heather said, "I don't know exactly. Belle said it would be unladylike of her to discuss it, but she was mad enough to spit. Now are you going to throw her out or not?"

"It's not that easy, even if I wanted to," I admitted. "Cragg drew up a new lease for her last night, and we both signed it with him acting as a witness."

Heather headed for the steps. "So she's here for good. I'm leaving then. I'll be out by the end of the month."

"Wait a second." I tried to explain that Sanora's lease only ran another two months, but Heather didn't give me the chance.

Now what had I gotten myself into?

I grabbed my clothes and headed downstairs. My regular coffee wasn't going to be enough to get me jump-started this morning; it was going to take some of Millie's special brew.

Instead of her usual warm greeting though, she faced me with a grim look as I approached the counter of The Crocked Pot.

"Good morning," I said. "I need something strong."

She slid a piece of paper across the counter without explanation.

"What's this," I asked.

"I think you should settle your bill before you order anything else."

It was a substantial amount, but I didn't doubt the total. I'd gotten lazy, taking many breakfasts and lunches at Millie's counter. It was a great deal easier than going out someplace, and I wasn't all that fond of eating alone up in my apartment. Still, it looked like I was going to have to make more of an effort, with the total now staring at me.

"I'm good for it," I said.

"Sorry, cash only until the bill's settled, landlord or not. And before you get any cute ideas about *my* lease, I just renewed it."

So that was what this was all about. I sat down hard on the stool and said, "I gather you're not pleased about Sanora coming back either."

"Harrison, how could you? She's already been thrown out once, and now you've let her back in."

"First of all, I didn't know she'd been thrown out. And second, her lease is only for two months. She's here on a trial basis. Would you mind telling me what she did that was so wrong?"

Millie eased her scowl for a moment. "I'm sorry, I shouldn't take it out on you, you didn't know. Heather came by, and she got me worked up all over again."

"So what happened?"

Millie said, "Coffee first, then we'll talk."

She poured me a mug of steaming coffee, and I took it gratefully. After a sip, I slid the bill back to her. "Here, put it on my tab. I left my wallet upstairs."

She laughed. "This one's on me." She tried to reach for the bill, but I snapped it up first. "I'm going to pay this tomorrow, as soon as Ann Marie brings me my check."

"There's no hurry," she said.

"I don't like having outstanding bills, Millie. I'm happy to settle it. Now tell me about Sanora."

"Well, you know me, I hate the spread of idle gossip, but there was money missing from a few tills, and someone saw Sanora coming out of shops she didn't have any business being in."

"So she was accused of stealing. What did the police say?"

"There was no evidence," she admitted reluctantly. "But

Gertie Braun swore up and down she was ninety-eight dollars short the day she saw Sanora slip out of her shop. She had the space Heather's in now, and she sold needlepoint supplies. Gertie's got quite a slick way with designs, but she was a nightmare for the business details. Sanora denied it, but Belle was itching for a fight when she issued her ultimatum."

"You heard it yourself?" I asked.

"It happened right over there," she said as she gestured to a table by the window. "I thought they were going to come to blows, Belle was so mad."

I shook my head as I took another sip of coffee. "So now I've let her back in. I wondered why Cragg insisted we sign the papers last night."

"It's no secret Gary Cragg's had a crush on Sanora Gaston since the day she came to River's Edge, married or not. It wouldn't surprise me if he's the one who put the thought of coming back into her head."

"So what am I going to do? Heather's talking about leaving."

"I'll have a chat with her after she's had a chance to cool down. I wouldn't worry about her skipping out, though. She signed her new lease the day I did. We're both going to be here for at least another year."

"She can still break it, can't she? You don't know how upset she was when she woke me up."

"I've got a good idea. She was building up a head of steam here before she came up to give you your wake-up call. There's something else you're forgetting. Aaron broke up with her to go back with Sanora, and once they were through for the second time, he didn't want her anymore. It's got to sting like the devil's tail to have to see the other woman at River's Edge. Stay out of Heather's way for the next few days and things will be fine."

"Thanks, Millie, I appreciate the advice, the information, and the tab. I'll talk to you later."

"Bye, Harrison. Sorry I was snippy with you."

"You? Snippy? I don't remember a thing."

I started for At Wick's End, but it was too early even for me. I noticed a pickup truck in front of The Pot Shot, quickly filling up with things from inside. Sanora was boxing up some of Aaron's things, and from the look of it, she'd been at it awhile. I'd just assumed she'd use his equipment and materials, but evidently I'd been wrong.

"Need a hand?" I asked.

"Thank goodness. I thought I was going to have to dismantle this thing before anyone offered to help. Grab an end, would you?"

I did as she asked, and was surprised to see we were removing the pottery wheel Aaron had been throwing at the night he'd died. It wasn't taking her long to get rid of it.

"You should have told me," I said as I grabbed the end with the motor mounted, surprised by how heavy the rig was.

"I don't even have to ask what you're talking about. Gertie Braun was senile if she thought I took that money, and Belle should never have believed her. I was innocent then, and I'm still innocent today."

"Why would you want to come back, knowing how folks around here feel about you?" I asked as I lifted my end onto the back of the truck. There was a scattering of tools in the truck bed, and I had to nudge aside a pair of wire cutters as I put my part of the pottery wheel down.

"I thought they'd be over it by now. I know Belle was your family, but it was wrong of her to throw me out. I love River's Edge. It's the perfect spot, as far as I'm concerned, and I'm not going to let a few cold shoulders drive me out. You're not going to try to break my lease, are you? Gary warned me you might."

"The lease we signed was binding," I stated simply.

"And after that, we'll see, right? That's all I ask, a chance to prove myself to you."

"Fair enough." I patted the old wheel. "What are you going to do with this?"

"It's going straight to the dump. I couldn't bear to have it around, knowing it was the cause of Aaron's death." She added, "Listen, thanks for the help, but I need to get back at it if I'm going to open in three days."

"Three days? Are you sure you'll be ready?"

"At the rate I'm going, I shouldn't have any problems. 'Bye, Harrison."

I watched her go back inside and started for At Wick's End, but as I did, I kept wondering why she didn't try to sell the electric wheel instead of getting rid of it at the dump. All it needed was a new power cord. Or was that why she was getting rid of it? Could it be incriminating evidence? She'd tried to explain away Aaron's presence at the electric wheel, but Markum and Heather had been adamant; Aaron Gaston didn't believe in them.

I'd seen a set of wire cutters among the tools on the back of the truck, so I walked back to it and grabbed them while Sanora was still working inside.

Rashly, I clipped the wire where it left the motor. I wanted a closer look at the insulation to see what I could find.

As I put the cutters back down, I heard a voice behind me, full of cold steel.

"Harrison? What are you doing?"

Six

I tried to discreetly coil the cord as I turned to face Sanora. "I dropped my watch when we loaded the truck," I said. I tucked the cord in the back of my shirt as I turned to face her. Thank goodness I'd worn a bulky top that morning, due more to the chill in the air than any thoughts of hiding things.

"What's wrong with your back?"

So I hadn't been all that slick in my movement. "I must have gotten into some poison ivy. It's been itching like crazy. Is that another box for the truck?"

She nodded, and I added, "Let me do that for you." I took it from her and placed it near where the power cord would have been. She might or might not notice it once she got to the dump. I was hoping she wouldn't, but if she did and asked me about it, I'd say I thought it had been gone when we'd moved the wheel. Let her think the sheriff took it. At least it had been coiled up and tied into a neat oval.

"Thanks again," she said as I walked away, hoping she didn't spot the extra bulge in my rugby shirt.

"No problem."

I walked past Heather's store and saw a large handmade sign in the window. In hard black letters, it said, MOVING SALE, and I felt my heart flutter in my throat. So it looked like she was following up on her threat to leave.

Not if I could help it. I didn't have all that many friends in Micah's Ridge, and I was in no mood to lose a single one of them. I wasn't going to let Heather go that easily.

I stashed the cord in my office, but not before examining it a little closer. I'd expected the edges to be frayed more around the cuts, but it looked cleaner than it should have. Maybe Pearly or Markum could take a look at it later. For now, I was glad it was in my office and not on the way to the dump.

I'd just tucked it behind a few boxes in the corner when I heard the front door open. Eve called out her greeting, and I said, "Be there in a minute."

I joined her by the cash register, fully expecting her to light into me, too, as soon as she found out about Sanora. I had two choices; wait till she heard about it on her own, or just get it over with. I chose the latter. I never have been one to be able to wait for the other shoe to drop.

"Eve, there's something you should know."

"About Sanora? I think it's a wonderful idea."

"You're not mad?" I asked.

"Harrison, you know I loved Belle like a sister, but she was too hard on Sanora. Gertie Braun was as likely as not to have tucked that cash in a book and forgotten it the next second. I tried to tell Belle that, but she wouldn't hear of it."

"Heather's threatening to move now," I said glumly.

"She's upset, that's natural, but I don't think she'll go, Harrison. She's happy here."

"Well, she was before all this happened. I'd hate to lose her."

Eve said, "Worried about replacing another tenant, or is there something deeper there?"

"I just hate the idea of losing a friend," I said, admitting nothing more.

"As do I. Take heart, things will work out for the best. I believe that with all my heart."

"I hope you're right."

It was a slow morning out front, and I needed to get ready for my next candlemaking lesson with Mrs. Jorgenson. She'd gotten the knack for dipping from the start, and if I knew my star student, she was practicing at home like mad on the basic techniques. I had to have something really special for her, and some research had given me a great idea. Eve had been my teacher from the beginning, and she was a pro at the basic techniques, but Mrs. J wouldn't stand for the simple after she'd conquered it, and I wanted to be ready for her.

I said, "If you can watch the front, there's something I need to take care of in the classroom."

"More monstrosities for our benefactress?" Eve had caught a glimpse of Mrs. Jorgenson's last lumpy candle and had found no charm in it at all.

"I've been studying a new technique," I said. "If you need me, just give me a yell."

She said lightly, "I believe I'll be able to handle anything that comes up. Go on and play."

"Hey, this is serious stuff," I said as I smiled at her.

I DID A tandem dip with beeswax as I'd shown Mrs. Jorgenson during her last lesson, alternating between two pairs to allow one to cool while the other was being dipped. When the first set was built up to about half an inch, I let it cool a few minutes, then grabbed both candles in one hand at their bases and twisted them together. I loved the look and set the twist aside. I repeated the same twist with the second pair, but this time I over-dipped the twist, not enough to obscure the curving lines, but enough to give it all a more solid look. I trimmed both bases before the wax hardened too much, then looked in the dipping can to see if I had enough wax to try another. There wasn't enough wax to dip another pair, but I wasn't going to stop dipping. I had an idea, remembering a candle I'd seen in one of my dozen reference books. I quickly dipped another half-inch taper just before the remaining wax started to congeal on the surface of the water. As soon as it was cool enough, I took out a rolling pin and flattened the candle on the tabletop, leaving a rounded base so it would still fit into a stand. The next step had looked tricky in the book, but I had to try it at least once. Grabbing the base in one hand and the exposed-wick end in the other, I gave the flattened candle a twist. It was outstanding; the taper looking elegant and extremely difficult to make. I was certain Mrs. Jorgenson would be pleased.

I'd just finished my cleanup when Eve came back. She studied my experiments without comment, though I noticed her gaze did linger a little longer on the flattened taper.

I smiled and said, "You should try it, it's lots of fun."

She said, "I'll stick with the traditional methods, thank you," though I could tell she was tempted. "You have a visitor."

"Is it somebody I'm going to be happy about seeing, or should I stay back here?"

Millie poked her head in. "Harrison Black, are you ducking me?"

"No, ma'am. I'm just hard at work."

"You missed the taste-test yesterday afternoon."

I'd forgotten all about Millie's offer to share her latest and greatest recipe. "Sorry."

"Nonsense, everyone deserves a little time off now and then. That's why I'm closed Sundays. It gives George and me time to get reacquainted." Millie's husband worked more jobs than any sane man would, but the two of them were happy with their arrangement, and far be it from me to interfere.

"Something smells wonderful," I said, looking at the basket tucked under her arm. A bright piece of gingham cloth covered the top, but it couldn't contain the heavenly aroma coming from beneath.

"That's why I'm here. Eve, would you like a sample?"

"I'll have to take a rain check, I'm losing ground on my diet as it is. Harrison, I'm meeting someone for lunch, so I may be a little late this afternoon."

"Take your time," I said. "I owe you."

After she was gone, Millie said, "Does our Eve have a new man in her life?"

"If she does, she hasn't said a word to me, and I'm not about to ask."

She laughed. "Such a big man, and a big coward, too."

"Hey, I never denied it. Now are you going to let me have a taste, or am I going to have steal that basket from you?"

"Never let it be said I led someone to a life a crime. Here, try one and tell me what you think."

She pulled back the cloth and I saw a batch of cranberry muffins, the bread shining like a wedding dress and the fat, crimson berries barely contained, bursting to get out. They were warm to the touch, and I took one and bit into it. It was absolutely the best muffin I'd ever had in my life. "What's in it?" I asked.

"Oh, cranberries of course, some flour and sugar, a little butter, things like that."

"In other words, don't ask." I took another bite and was startled to find that I'd polished it off.

"So what do you think?"

I stroked my chin and said, "Well, it's really hard to say based on such a small sample. I'd better try another one."

She held the basket out of my reach. "You've already used that on me, you rascal. Honestly, do you like them?"

"They are spectacular," I admitted. "Does that buy me another one?"

"I don't want to spoil your appetite," she said, laughing softly.

"Have a heart. You heard Eve, she might not be back till tonight."

"Oh pooh, of course they're all for you. Thanks, Harrison, I trust your palate."

"You shouldn't," I said.

"And why not?"

"I love everything you make." I took another muffin out, had a bite of it, and said, "If I could get upstairs to my apartment, I'd grab some cold milk and be set. I don't suppose you could . . ."

She laughed and said, "This isn't a catering service, you know. Now I've got to get back to The Crocked Pot. I locked up so I could bring these by."

"Thanks again, Millie, you've got another winner here."

Before she could leave, I added, "Did you see the sign on Heather's shop? She's having a moving sale."

"Oh dear, I never thought it would come to that. I'd better talk to her."

"Let me know what you find out, would you?"

"If I have any luck at all, I will. If you don't hear from me, it's not good news."

Five minutes later the chime rang over the door and Sanora Gaston walked in with a tall glass of milk. "This is from Millie. She said you'd understand."

I took it from her and had a healthy swallow. "Thanks, that was great. Sorry you had to deliver it to me."

"I didn't mind. Harrison, I came by to see if you'd like to have lunch with me today."

"I'd like to, but Eve just left, and there's nobody to watch the shop till she gets back. How about a rain check?"

"You've got it. I guess I'll take Tick up on her invitation. She wants to welcome me back."

"That's sweet of her," I said. "Sorry I didn't think of it first."

"There will be plenty of time. We'll do it later."

The rest of the day dragged through starts and sputters, never anything steady but accumulating to a healthy total as I started to run the day's report off the register. Eve had been cryptic about her lunch after she'd returned, but I could tell something pleasant had happened while she'd been gone. She scooted out the door two minutes after I locked it, another sign that something was up. Eve was usually a stickler for our closing routine, but today she obviously had something else on her mind.

I was just walking out with the deposit when Erin walked up. "You're closed? I got here as fast I as I could."

"Tell you what, let me open back up and I'll give you the nickel tour."

"I hate when people come right when I'm closing. Harrison, I wouldn't do that to you."

"But I'm offering," I said as I opened the door and held it for her. "Come in and take the grand tour."

She stepped inside and I locked the door behind her. "I hope you don't mind, but I don't want anybody else wandering in. Not that I'm trying to get you alone. No, that didn't sound right either. Would you feel more comfortable if I left it unlocked?"

Erin smiled at my stammering. "I think I'll be safe enough with you. Besides, I've got some Mace in my pocket if you get out of line."

"No, ma'am, you don't have to worry about me." I added, "Is there anything in particular you'd like to see, or would you like a quick overview of it all?"

"If you don't have anything pressing, I'd love to see it all."

"I'd be delighted. Why don't we start up front with our displays so you can see the different types of candles we make, then we'll take a stroll through the aisles." I showed her some of the hand-dipped candles I'd made and just displayed, along with poured candles, some rolled ones from sheets of wax, gel candles, floating candles, and braided ones. She was particularly fascinated with a carved candle that looked as if it had been dipped in the world of fairies and sprites. "Wow, did you actually make this one?"

"That's beyond my talent as of yet. My Great-Aunt Belle did. At Wick's End was hers before I inherited it."

"She was wonderful, wasn't she?" Erin said, studying the piece.

"In more than just her candlemaking," I said.

Erin nodded, then we walked through the shelves until we reached the classroom in back.

"Is this where you actually make them?"

"It is. We teach classes, too." I picked up one of the braided candles I'd just made and handed it to her.

She asked, "Is this another one of Belle's creations? It's absolutely beautiful."

I smiled. "That happens to be one of mine. I'm glad you like it."

"I love it, but it looks a little complex for me. What's the easiest way to start making candles?"

I led her to the shelves with packets of sheet wax and wicks, ready for rolling. "These are fun, easy, and they burn great. It's a wonderful place to start."

"I'll take one." She studied the packet, then said, "I was going to ask for a lesson, but this says the instructions are inside."

I shrugged. "I'd be happy to supplement them, if you're interested. Strictly teacher to student."

She thought about it a second or two, then said, "Why don't I try my hand at this myself and see how I do? What do I owe you?"

"I've got an idea," I said as I took the packet from her and grabbed a bag. "Why don't we barter? You come by for candle supplies, and I'll grab a kayak now and then."

"I'm all about bartering," she said enthusiastically. "My hairdresser loves to canoe with her boyfriend, so we trade, too."

I wrapped the braided candle she'd admired and slipped it into the bag as well.

She asked, "Hey, why did you do that? All I expected was the kit."

"These are on the house. I can always make more."

"Are you sure? That's awfully generous of you."

"I'm positive."

She took the bag, then said, "Thank you, kind sir, I do appreciate that. I'll burn it tonight." She thought about it a second, then added, "That's kind of tacky of me, isn't it? You probably like them to be displayed, don't you?"

"Candles are made for burning. I've got a friend who bakes, and she'd be insulted if you didn't actually eat her creations."

Erin nodded, then lingered by the register. She read aloud the week's quote I'd printed out and posted the day before.

" 'My candle burns at both ends; but ah, my foes, and oh, my friends—it gives a lovely light.' I know that one. She's one of my favorites."

"Put the poet's name on a slip of paper and you'll be eligible for the drawing." I'd started the candle-quote contest the week before, and Eve had been amazed how many of our regulars had taken the chance to win a ten-dollar gift certificate to the shop.

I saw Erin write "Edna St. Vincent Millay" on the paper, and she even added "A Few Figs from Thistles" on it. She was right on the money.

"I put my phone number on there, too," she said.

"That's great. Good luck. I'll call you if you're the winner."

She frowned a second, then nodded. "Okay. Thanks again for the tour, Harrison."

"You're welcome. Let me know how your candles turn out."

"I will." Erin lingered at the door a moment, then watched

as I locked up behind her. I'd been tempted to ask her out, but my rule was firm. I'd asked her once, and she'd declined. If she was interested in anything else, it was going to be up to her. I didn't have all that much time in my life for dating anyway, not with running At Wick's End and trying to keep River's Edge afloat as well, and my ego could only take so much rejection. Still, she'd given me her phone number, that was something.

I made out the deposit for the day and was locking the front door when I remembered the power cord I'd cut off Aaron's pottery wheel. After slipping it into one of our bags, I locked up again and headed to the bank for my nightly deposit. I'd lost a deposit once because of my carelessness, but it had taken only one time to teach me that particular lesson. I drove to the bank, thought about grabbing something to eat, then decided my waistline and my wallet could both use some home-cooking, even if it did mean spaghetti or a sandwich.

Cragg was just locking up his office when I walked upstairs. I normally do all I can to avoid confrontations, but he'd tried to railroad me into accepting Sanora Gaston back to River's Edge, and I wasn't about to let him get away with it.

Seven

"I don't like what you did," I said without preface.

"What are you referring to?" he asked in his deliberate and sonorous tone.

"You had to know how folks around here felt about Sanora. Why didn't you warn me?"

"Warn you of what, idle gossip, rumor, and rampant speculation? She was ill-accused, Harrison, and I wasn't about to perpetuate the myth. She belongs at River's Edge."

I shook my head. How in the world had I been dense enough to actually believe I could win an argument with a lawyer? "I know this is an argument I'm not going to win. I'm just glad I didn't sign her up to a long-term lease."

"So you've made your mind up already? You're not even going to give her a chance, are you?"

I thought about it a second, then said, "I haven't made my mind up about anything. I just wish I'd had all the information before I made my decision."

That appeased him somewhat. "Just be fair, that's all I ask. She deserves at least that."

"As do we all," I said and slipped inside before Cragg had the chance to get the last word in. Had I meant what I'd said? Was there a chance in the world I would trade Sanora's presence at River's Edge for Heather's? If it came down to keeping one tenant and losing the other, was that a decision I was willing to make? I didn't want to lose Heather, either as a tenant or a friend, but I also wasn't about to let anyone dictate my leasing policies to me. Right or wrong, River's Edge was mine to run.

I just hoped it didn't come down to losing either one.

There was a knock at my door, and I knew Cragg hadn't been satisfied in letting me end our conversation. As I opened it, I said, "I told you I'd think about it."

Markum was there, leaning against the wall just outside my door. "That's all a man can ask. I'll leave you, then."

I said, "Come on in. I thought you were Cragg."

Markum's lip curled in disgust. "That's the meanest thing I ever heard you say, Harrison."

"You know what I meant."

The big man came in and made a stab at reining in his wild black hair with a meaty hand. "Sorry to interrupt, but I came by to see what the sheriff had to say."

"Not much," I admitted, retelling the conversation I'd had with Morton and the fact that Sanora had taken the wheel to the dump, without mentioning my theft.

Markum said, "So that's that, then. We're left without any evidence. I thought, a little too late, about that pottery wheel. When I asked Sanora if I could buy it from her this afternoon, she told me it was already gone."

I jiggled the bag in my hand. "The wheel's gone, but I got the cord before she could get rid of it."

Markum slapped me on the back, nearly knocking me back. "Harrison Black, I'll make a salvage man out of you yet. Let's see it."

I handed the cord over. "I got my fingerprints all over it."

Markum took it and said, "Come down the hall with me. I want to get a better look at it."

I followed him out of my apartment and locked the door behind me. Once we were in his office, Markum turned on a light that circled a magnifying glass. It was the size of a coffee cup saucer, and there was no doubt he could indeed get a closer look than the naked eye.

"That's quite a rig," I said.

"It's useful at times, no doubt about that," he muttered as he unwrapped the cord and studied it, inch by inch. I busied myself watching him for a time, but after a while my gaze shifted to some of the travel posters up in his office. He'd added a new one since I'd been there last, one of a steam-driven engine racing through a mountain pass, the fog lying low in the autumn hills and a blanket of patchwork colors draping it.

"So," Markum said as he moved the light's swivel head out of his way.

"It was an accident after all," I said.

"I doubt it, but we're not going to be able to prove it by this. Whoever did this was slick, I'll give them that. Look at this."

I studied the section under the lens and saw the jagged tearing of the cord's insulation. "What am I looking at? It's about what I expected."

Markum took a pencil point and as it slid under the magnification, it grew twenty times in size. "Look here, at the very start of the tear. What do you see?"

"The line is cleaner than the rest," I said.

Markum nodded, then switched off the light. "I suspect the first cut was made with a knife, then the gap was rubbed over a piece of wood until the edges softened."

"So let's take this to Morton. He's got to listen now."

Markum shook his head. "I doubt it. The police work by something called the chain of evidence, and this one's been lost. What's to say we didn't make that little nick ourselves? Even if he believed us, it's not exactly overwhelming evidence, is it?"

"So what do we do?"

Markum thought about it a second, then said, "We watch, and we wait. I've a feeling this particular drama hasn't played to its end just yet."

"You know, it might help if I had the slightest idea what you were talking about."

Markum laughed so loud it nearly shook the panes of glass in his office. "Harrison, I've spent too many hours alone talking to myself for lack of decent company. You keep your eyes open during the day, and I'll do the same at night. Between the two of us, we'll have someone at River's Edge watching all the time."

"Do you think Aaron's death had something to do with the complex?"

Markum shrugged. "I'm not sure what to think just yet. I'm afraid there's nothing else we can do about it right now." He started to hand the cord back to me, then hesitated. "Do you mind if I keep this?"

"Be my guest."

He nodded, opened the safe in his closet and slammed it shut. "There, I feel better about it already."

My stomach rumbled, and Markum said, "I'd say you were late for a bite of supper."

"I'm hungry, I admit it. Care to join me?"

He laughed. "I had breakfast an hour ago, my friend. We work on different schedules, in so many ways. Good night, Harrison."

"Good morning," I said, and he grinned broadly at me. Markum was more of a mystery after every conversation I had with him than he had been before. Yet again I promised myself that one of these days, I'd surprise us both and take him up on his offer to take part in one of his salvage operations. It would most likely be many things, but I doubted boring would be among them.

It was frustrating not being able to do anything more about Aaron's murder. No matter what Sheriff Morton thought, I believed just as much as Markum did that Aaron Gaston had been helped along.

Proving it was going to be another matter altogether.

I HEATED A can of soup, made a sandwich, and was just sitting down to eat when someone knocked at the door of my apartment. As I walked over to see who it was, I wondered about Belle's decision to live on the property in the only apartment in River's Edge. There was no doubt it was a time-saver on the commute, since I was living right over the top of At Wick's End, and it was great not having any rent or utilities to pay, but the downside was that it was extremely difficult to ever get away from it all. It explained Belle's retreat on the roof, and why I'd been spending more and more time up there lately. But when winter finally set in, what was I going to do? I couldn't see going to the refuge when there were icy winds coming off the river, let alone snow. I'd have to find someplace else to get away.

Pearly Gray was at the door, running a hand through his luxuriant gray hair.

"Sorry I'm late," he said as he stepped inside. There was a clipboard in one hand.

"Late? For what?"

He glanced at my small dining table and said, "You forgot about our meeting, didn't you? We can do this tomorrow, there's nothing urgent."

Then it hit me. We'd decided to have a meeting once a month so I could keep up with what was going on at River's Edge, and I knew without looking at my calendar that tonight was the date we'd scheduled. Pearly was too precise to have ever forgotten.

"Do you mind if I eat while we talk? I can offer you a sandwich if you're hungry." It was time to go shopping again. I'd opened my last can of soup, and my cupboard was decidedly bare.

"No, I ate hours ago. If you're sure you want to do this, I don't mind keeping you company."

"Excellent. At least let me get you something to drink." I peered into the refrigerator and quickly inventoried my meager choices. "I've got some Bo's sweet tea and some orange juice. I can offer you water, too."

He shook his head and smiled slightly. "Harrison, there's an art to living on your own. It's taken me years to master it, and I'd be happy to share some of my techniques for single habitation."

"I'm fine, thanks. You just caught me before grocery day."

He nodded. "Of course. Shall we get started?"

"Sounds good to me." As much as I liked my erudite handyman, I'd been hoping for some time alone.

He glanced at the clipboard and said, "First of all, with The Pot Shot's space now occupied, we're back at full capacity."

"What do you think of me letting Sanora come back to River's Edge?"

Pearly said, "Harrison, frankly it's none of my business. She should be a good tenant if her past history is any indication."

"You mean you aren't going to disapprove *or* scold me? Everyone else has expressed an opinion quick enough."

Pearly leaned back in his chair. "River's Edge is yours to do with as you see fit. I didn't get involved when Belle evicted Sanora, and I'm certainly not going to meddle now."

"Thanks for that," I said sincerely. "How is she getting along?"

"Tick's taken her under her wing, I'm happy to say. They made their peace rather quickly. Sanora and Heather are still at odds. I'm worried we might lose her, Harrison, regardless of her lease."

"I'm worried, too. Anything we can do about it?"

"I'm afraid it's out of our hands. I'm concerned about her, though, and I'm not afraid to admit it."

There was something in his eyes and the catch in his voice that told me Pearly wasn't saying everything he was thinking.

I said, "I know I haven't known Heather as long as you have, but I care about her, too. There's something else, isn't there?"

Pearly stared at his hands for the longest time, then said, "I've lost more than one night's sleep wanting to tell you something, but for the life of me I can't decide if I should."

I waited him out, letting him decide for himself.

After a full minute of silence, he said, "I hope what I'm about to tell you will be kept in strictest confidence."

"I already know Heather and Aaron were seeing each other," I said.

"As does the rest of River's Edge. No, this is about the night Aaron died."

That certainly got my attention. "What happened?"

"It may be nothing, in fact, it probably is, but I saw Heather out and about that night. I watched her from a window upstairs and saw her in the parking lot staring at Aaron's shop. She stood there the longest time without moving, as if she was waiting for something to happen, something she dreaded."

"When exactly was this?"

He sighed heavily, then said, "Ten minutes before the power went off."

I took some time to digest what he'd told me. Could Heather have had something to do with Aaron's death? I'd known her less than a month, but I considered her beyond an act of murder. But I hadn't known her when she'd been with Aaron. Could his rejection of her have driven her to ending his life?

"It's probably nothing, isn't it?" he asked hopefully.

"I wish I could tell you that, I truly do."

Pearly said, "I should have kept it to myself. Now I've passed my nightmares on to you."

"If it happened at River's Edge, I need to know about it. I rely on you to keep me informed, and I thank you for sharing this with me. Is there anything else I need to know about?"

"As far as the building is concerned? I'm nervous about the wiring. I know I've expressed my concerns before, but it bears repeating. We should be on a ground-fault interrupter for the entire complex. What happened to Aaron could leave us open to a lawsuit."

"We can't afford any upgrades right now, you know that as well as I do. Besides, I don't see how what happened to Aaron could have been our fault."

"Most likely you're right, I worry too much." That was patently false, as Pearly was one of the most serene men I'd ever known.

"So that's it," I said.

He said, "Harrison, you certainly don't have to, but you're most welcome to join me on my rounds tonight. I like to walk around the property and make certain all is as it should be on the grounds."

I wanted to say no, but how could I, when I was keeping Pearly from his own personal life? "Just let me grab a jacket."

"There's a chill in the air tonight, no doubt about it."

We walked down the stairs and out into the night. Pearly said, "I'm afraid I let my batteries go dead in my flashlight."

"We'll manage," I said as a breeze from the river nudged us. I was glad I'd remembered my coat and zipped it up against the wind.

"Hey there," he suddenly called out into the night, and it took me a second to spot the person he was hailing. The sound of Pearly's voice made the figure jerk, but it was too dark and we were too far away for me to see who it was. I saw the stranger's hand go back, and for an instant I thought they might have a gun. Then the glass window at The Pot Shot shattered into a thousand pieces as the alarm went off inside.

Pearly and I raced after the culprit, but it was impossible to find them in the darkness.

Panting and nearly out of breath, Pearly caught up with me under a nearby streetlight as the taillights of a car disappeared. "Did you get a license plate number?" he asked.

"No, it happened too fast. I didn't even see what kind of car it was," I admitted. Some keen observer I'd turned out to be.

"That brings up one more item on my list."

"What's that?" I asked as we walked back to River's Edge to survey the damage.

"We could use security lights around the building, with some motion sensors."

"I'll call Ann Marie in the morning. Whether it's in the budget or not, we'll find the money for that."

He patted my shoulder. "Now let's go see if we can clean up that mess."

I phoned the vandalism in to the police department, and once the dispatcher found that there was no one hurt, she promised to get someone out there first thing in the morning. The virus that was going through the police department had left them severely short-staffed, and she was frank about their nonemergency response time.

It took us an hour to sweep up all the glass and mount a sheet of plywood over the hole until I could call the insurance company and a glazier in the morning. We found a jagged piece of brick among the debris, and though I doubted it would yield fingerprints, I still picked it up with my handkerchief and set it aside. An errant thought raced through my mind. Was it possible Heather had thrown the brick, instead of a vandal? No, I knew she despised Sanora, but I couldn't see her acting out so destructively.

Before we started cleaning up, I'd asked Pearly, "Should we call Sanora and tell her what happened?"

"There's nothing she can do about it tonight. Why ruin a night of rest for her, since it may be the last one she gets for a while?"

"Why do you say that?"

Pearly said, "Wouldn't you say this is a message for her? We saw for ourselves that it wasn't exactly a random act of violence, now didn't we?"

"It did seem pretty deliberate. Can you start on those lights in the morning?"

"I'll put it at the top of my list. You might also consider mounting some security cameras around the perimeter."

"Even if I could afford it, I'm not interested in living in an armed camp. Tell you what, I'll see if Morton can step up his patrols out here if anyone ever shows up tomorrow."

We surveyed our work, then locked the store back up. Pearly said, "Well, if there's nothing else, it's been a long day."

"Thanks, Pearly. For everything."

He shrugged. "It's my pleasure, as well as my responsibility. I'll see you in the morning, Harrison."

I saw him drive off, then mounted the stairs to my apartment. I hoped there were no more emergencies that night, because I was through answering my door. Ultimately, it always seemed to lead to nothing but trouble.

Eight

THE next morning, I'd barely been in At Wick's End ten minutes when there was an urgent staccato knocking on the front door. Some mornings were like that, when impatient candlemakers had to get their supplies before I was ready to open the shop. I was tempted to let them in early, since I was already there, but Eve had taught me that it was setting a bad trend, and in all honesty, we were open enough hours to fit just about anyone's schedule.

It was impossible to concentrate on putting together my supply order with that constant barrage though, so I gave up and walked out front.

Sanora was there, and from the expression on her face, she was loaded for bear.

"What happened?" she demanded as quickly as I could open the door.

I said, "Calm down. There was some vandalism last night. Pearly and I put up the plywood until I could call a glazier."

"Why didn't you call me, Harrison? It *is* my store, isn't it?"

I nodded. "It's also my building, and I'm responsible for what happens to it." I tried to keep my voice calm and level. She had every right to be upset. The vandalism was a violation, and she no doubt felt like lashing out at anybody or anything within range.

"You should have called me," she said, quieting down a little.

"I thought about it, but why ruin your night? Pearly and I saw it happen."

"So who did it? Did the police arrest them?"

I admitted, "It was dark, and they got away. We're putting in security lights over the next couple of days. I know it might feel like we're locking the barn door after the horse is gone, but it should help from now on. I'm truly sorry it happened."

The rest of the steam went out of her. She said softly, "Who would do this? Is someone trying to run me off?"

"I honestly don't know."

Sanora took a deep breath, then said, "Well I'm not going to give them the satisfaction. I'm staying, Harrison."

"I'm glad to have you here, Sanora." And it was true. What had happened in the past wasn't a part of my time at River's Edge. She'd been an ideal tenant since coming back, working hard and keeping out of trouble. Her check even cleared the first time through, something I couldn't say about some of my other folks. For all the money Tick took in at her antique shop, it was a rare check indeed that went through the first time, no matter how steep I made my fee for bouncing them.

Then I remembered how quickly Sanora had gotten rid of the evidence in Aaron's death. Would an innocent person do that? Was she being efficient, or was it something much more sinister? The problem was, I liked her, and I was afraid it might be clouding my judgment.

She studied me a moment, then said, "Next time, call me. Day or night."

"I promise."

Sanora nodded, satisfied, then said, "As soon as I get my hands on Pearly, I'll read him the riot act, too." She shook her head, then added, "Thanks for cleaning up."

"It was the least we could do after letting them get away. Tell you what, why don't I buy you breakfast?"

"I appreciate the offer, but I'm not all that sure Millie wants me here. This vandalism has made her frosty toward me again."

I shrugged. "It's your call, but I thought you just said no one was going to run you off."

Sanora shrugged. "I'm willing to face her if you are."

"Let's go," I said, then locked the shop door behind me as we headed for The Crocked Pot.

As expected, Millie wasn't all that thrilled seeing Sanora with me. "What can I get you?"

"Two Rise and Shiners sound great." Millie baked the most wonderful muffins, as big as dinner plates and tender as a baby's laughter.

I said, "Did you hear about the break-in attempt last night?"

Millie, carefully keeping her gaze away from Sanora, said, "I saw the plywood."

"Pearly and I were there when it happened. We both chased the bad guy, but he got away."

Sanora asked, "It was a man, then?"

I shrugged. "Might have been. Of course, it could have just as easily been a woman."

Despite her pressed lips, Millie said, "Now there's a description the police can use."

"Hey, what can I say? It was dark. We're putting in security lights the next day or two."

"Belle had always planned to add them. She just never got around to it." Millie put our muffins and coffees on two separate trays, and I was about to tell her to put it on my tab when Sanora slid a ten-dollar bill over the counter.

Surprised, I said, "Hey, I invited you to breakfast, remember?"

"You can pick up the next one."

Millie made change without a word, then busied herself behind the counter as we found a table near the window. I always enjoyed watching the water, and now that I'd been out on it in one of Erin's kayaks, the river had taken on a new meaning for me. If I could manage it, I wanted to get back out there as soon as possible. One trip out on the water and it was already getting in my blood.

After some small talk and most of our breakfast, I asked, "So is this going to slow down your opening?"

"I'm set for tomorrow, whether the glass is replaced by then or not." She lowered her voice and added, "I can't afford to stay closed that long, Harrison. That's why I've been working like a demon over here. I'm counting on enough of Aaron's old customers to join mine to make this work, but it's hard to say what will happen."

"Do you have any press coverage or ads planned?" I'd just recently started looking into promotion opportunities for At Wick's End. It was nearly impossible to run a small business, I was discovering, without letting the world know you were out there.

"Maybe later, but I didn't have time to do anything but the basics. This was all kind of sudden. Who would have believed Aaron would die like he did?"

That was an opening I just couldn't resist. I took a last sip of coffee, then asked, "Have you considered the possibility that Aaron's death wasn't an accident?"

She dropped the muffin onto her plate. "What are you talking about?"

I'd committed myself, and was starting to regret the bluntness of what I was about to say before it was even out of my mouth. "That power cord could have been frayed on purpose, and it's a mighty big stretch to think he kicked over a bucket of water at exactly the wrong time in exactly the wrong place."

Sanora bolted out of her chair as if it had been electrified. "Are you insane, or just incredibly cruel? What comes next, an accusation? Aaron and I were friends, even after our marriage broke up. I didn't want him dead."

She stumbled toward the door and nearly ran Cragg down on her way out. He gave me a quick look of venomous displeasure, then followed her out.

Millie came over and said, "I should apologize to you. I never thought you'd bring her here to grill her."

"Millie, I asked her something I had no right to, and Sanora was right. I was out of line."

"Hey, where are you going?" she called out as I headed for the door.

"I'm going to apologize," I said.

Sanora was at The Pot Shot, and Cragg was there holding her hand.

I said, "I need to talk to you."

"She's through talking to you," the attorney said firmly.

"Okay, she doesn't have to talk, but I need her to hear this. Sanora, I'm sorry. I was out of line."

"You've said your piece," Cragg said, the dismissal thick in his voice. "Now go."

"It's okay, Gary," Sanora said, dabbing at her eyes with his embroidered linen handkerchief.

"Sanora, I'm sorry. I didn't mean to imply anything."

"I overreacted, Harrison. You didn't say anything everyone else here wasn't already thinking. I loved Aaron in my own way. There was no way I'd wish him harm."

Cragg said stiffly, "If I'm no longer needed here, I've got to prepare for a case today."

He brushed past me with barely a nod.

"I didn't mean to run him off," I said after he was gone.

"Don't worry, you couldn't get rid of Gary with a

blowtorch if he really wanted to stay. I'm afraid he's got a bit of a crush on me."

"A bit? It looked like more than that to me."

Sanora dabbed at her eyes, then said, "You wouldn't believe how furious he was when Aaron and I started dating again. I thought he was going to have a stroke."

"He took it that hard?"

"Gary asked me out a dozen times, but I kept telling him we were just friends. Then he saw me with Aaron last week at The Shallows and misunderstood completely. I never got the chance to explain."

"He *is* overprotective of you, isn't he?"

Sanora said, "And there was no reason for it, either. Aaron was even seeing someone else, though he admitted he was about to break it off. My ex-husband was much better at acquiring girlfriends than he was in keeping them." She looked around the shop, then said, "Listen, I would appreciate it if you'd call the glazier for me and tell them it's a rush job. It's as dark as a tomb in here. Oh, no." She bolted for the bathroom in back and I let myself out. A tomb is exactly what the shop had been, if just for a few hours.

Instead of going back to At Wick's End, I walked down the steps to the river. It was the perfect place to think before the stores at River's Edge started to fill up. It was hard to wipe the image of Gary Cragg out of my mind as he'd hovered over Sanora. Her admission that he'd had a crush on her started me thinking. Could the attorney have frayed that cord himself in an effort to get rid of an obstacle in his way? If he'd seen Aaron and Sanora cozying up at a restaurant, it might have been enough to drive him into action. I wished I could say that Cragg was above murder, but I honestly didn't know if I believed it.

I was still thinking about it when Tick jogged up. "You're out early," I said as she stretched beside me.

"I jog three miles every morning. You should join me sometime."

"I like my exercise at a more leisurely pace," I admitted.

"What happened to the window?" she asked as she looked at the pottery shop.

"We had a little vandalism last night."

Tick shook her head. "What is this world coming to? Well, I've got to grab a quick shower before I open the shop. See you later."

She started to go when I said, "Tick, I appreciate you spending time with Sanora. You might want to drop in on her before you open."

"I'll do just that. See you later, Harrison."

I got up and brushed off my jeans. I still had that order to call in before we opened, and if I left it till the last minute, Eve would certainly scold me about it. Sometimes it was hard to remember that I was the one who owned At Wick's End and she was the employee.

As I walked past Heather's shop, there was a new sign in the window. CLOSED TILL FURTHER NOTICE. Now when had she done that? That sign hadn't been there yesterday afternoon, I would have noticed it. Could she have done it this morning, and I'd missed seeing her? Another thought struck me, one I didn't want to admit. Was it possible she'd posted it last night, just before hurling that brick through Sanora's window?

No, I couldn't believe it, not of my friend.

But the possibility refused to go away.

I NEEDN'T HAVE worried about Eve noticing any lapses of my responsibilities. She was in her own world as we opened the store and welcomed our customers.

Sheriff Morton came in an hour after we opened. He looked pale and there was a sheen of sweat on his brow, though it was still cool outside. "Harrison, you have a second?"

"Absolutely," I told him. I turned to Eve and said, "I won't be long."

She nodded curtly, then went back to the customer she was helping.

Outside, Morton said, "She's all full of cheer, isn't she?"

"Actually, this is one of her good days. So what do you think about the window?"

"It looks like you and Pearly did a good job patching it, but I'd get the glass man in here if you want to keep Sanora off your back. She can be a real pain in the neck when she wants to be."

"You know Aaron's ex-wife?"

Morton said, "Let's just say we went out a few times and leave it at that, can we? I got the brick from her, but it's not going to do any good. I found a pile of them around the back of the building. You really should get that cleaned up, Harrison, you don't want rats moving in on you."

"I've got it on my list," I admitted. "There's no chance of fingerprints?"

"Not off that. It probably wasn't even planned. Some kids were probably up to mischief and it was Sanora's unlucky night."

"There was just one person there. Pearly and I saw him. Or her, we really couldn't be certain."

"I guess I won't be calling on you as a witness," he said. "Listen, there's nothing I can do here. Sorry, but I don't have a thing to go on, and I'm trying to hold down the fort until some of my people get back." He coughed a few times. "Blast it all, I think I'm coming down with it myself. Just what I need, a case of the crud when everything's falling down around my ears."

"You'd better take care of yourself. Why don't you see if Millie has any chicken soup? It's got to help."

"It didn't do the chickens much good, did it?" He coughed again, then added, "I've got to go."

"Hope you feel better," I called out as he headed for his squad car, but I couldn't be sure he'd even heard me. It looked like a great time to commit a crime in Micah's Ridge, with half the force down with the flu. I just hoped the criminals didn't catch wind of it.

Eve was talking on the telephone when I walked back into At Wick's End, and from the sound of it, things weren't going all that well. There were no customers in the shop, so I kept myself busy straightening shelves until she got off.

"Is everything all right?" I asked. Her face was a frozen mask.

"It's just wonderful," she said, the words dripping with sarcasm.

"Listen, I'm not trying to pry, but if you need someone to talk to, I'm right here."

She started to say something, then bit it back. Her expression did ease somewhat when she said, "I'll be fine. At least it's not a mistake I have to keep paying for. It's over."

Now what in the world could I say to that? "Anyway, I'm here if you need me."

She nodded. "I know, but it's nothing I care to discuss. I know it's early, but if you don't mind, I'd like to take my lunch." She blew out a gust of air, then said plaintively, "Truthfully, I'd rather not work today. Do you mind if I take a vacation day?"

"Go ahead, I've got things covered here."

As Eve grabbed her jacket from our shared office, she said, "You don't have to tell me that. You've been working so hard since you came, you're ready to handle it all."

"Come on, I figure there's a lot more you can teach me."

She sighed, then said, "Perhaps, but I doubt it. Goodbye, Harrison."

"See you tomorrow," I called out, but she just waved as the door closed behind her.

I surely hoped I would see her tomorrow. I hadn't been in the candlemaking business all that long, and I certainly wasn't ready to run At Wick's End without Eve. Could I muddle along with it if she left? Most likely, but it wouldn't be easy. Hopefully the day off was all she needed, but with Eve, I couldn't be entirely sure.

I should have packed my lunch, but then I hadn't known earlier that Eve was going to bail out on me. There was only one thing I could do as my stomach rumbled. I scrawled out a sign that said, BACK IN 5 MINUTES, taped it to the door and jogged down to Millie's for a quick bite.

There was a line of customers, including Sanora and Tick standing close together. Tick called me over. "Harrison, care to join us?"

"I'd love to, but I'm watching the shop by myself. I'll come back later."

Millie spotted me and said, "Harrison, come here a second."

I walked to the counter, nodding my apologies to the folks in line. "I can wait."

"I'm not worried about your lunch, I'll send something down a little later. I want to talk to you about Heather's sign." She'd said the last in a near-whisper as she worked at filling orders, no doubt trying to keep the news from Sanora.

I stopped her. "We can talk about it when you bring me something later."

She frowned a moment, then agreed. "I won't be long, Mrs. Quimby is helping me out."

"When did you hire her?" I asked.

"The second I found out Heather let her go. I've known her for years, and honestly, I can use the help."

"It sounds serious, doesn't it?" I asked. Mrs. Quimby was devoted to Heather and Esmeralda. If Heather had actually fired her from her part-time position, she really must be poised to break her lease and move.

What had I done by letting Sanora come to River's Edge?

"We'll talk soon," Millie said, and I went back to At Wick's End to wait on her. I was more interested in the conversation than the lunch, but I wouldn't turn down either one. It looked like things were changing yet again at River's Edge, and not for the better.

Nine

"I don't think it's as dire as you believe, Harrison," Millie told me as I finished the last of my sandwich an hour later. "There's hope yet."

For once I was happy the foot traffic in At Wick's End was light. I needed to eat, and just as important, I had to talk to Millie. Pearly may have been the one who kept me up to date on the physical aspects of River's Edge, but Millie knew the complex's heart.

"How can you say that?" I asked. "She fired Mrs. Quimby and put a moving-sale sign up in her window. It can't get much darker than that."

"I spoke with Vera at length, and she said Heather was still unsure about what she was going to do."

"Who's Vera?" I asked.

"You know, Mrs. Quimby."

"Vera is Mrs. Quimby's first name?" I asked as I finished off my sweet tea.

"Why yes. Why does that surprise you?"

"I just never thought about it before. She's been

'Mrs. Quimby' since I first met her. I never really thought about her having a first name."

"I think Vera's a perfectly lovely name. Now let's get back to Heather. Are you adamant about keeping Sanora at River's Edge, or is there any chance you'll change your mind?"

I stood, wadded the wrapping paper from my lunch, and threw it into the trashcan. "We signed a lease, but it only runs until the end of next month."

Millie started to say something, but I quickly added, "Her renewal is not going to depend on Heather, as much as I'd like her to stay. Millie, I'm not being hardnosed about this, but Belle left River's Edge to me, not the entire tenants association. I have to do what I think is best. Would I have liked to have known about all this before I agreed to let Sanora reopen the pottery shop? Absolutely. But Cragg never hinted at it as he was twisting my arm. Why isn't anyone mad at him?"

"Gary is what he has always been. I'm sure he tried to finesse his playmates in preschool, and he's not about to change."

"So Heather's leaving if Sanora stays. I don't want that to happen, and I'll do whatever I can to prevent it, short of evicting Sanora."

"So we're at a standoff, is that it?"

"My hands are tied," I said. "If I had a chance to talk to her, I might be able to change her mind."

"I wouldn't mind speaking with her myself, but Vera told me Heather was leaving town for a few weeks. She's got a friend in Charlotte she's going to be staying with."

"Well, that's a good sign, at least."

"What do you mean?"

I said, "Think about it. If she's not in town and Mrs. Quimby is working for you, Heather can't start selling off her stock."

"I suppose."

The bell above my door chimed and I saw Mrs. Simms walk in. I told Millie, "I'd love to help, but I've got to keep my eyes on this woman. She steals for the fun of it, but I haven't been able to catch her with the goods yet."

"I'll leave you to it."

Millie gave Mrs. Simms a wide berth as she left the store, and I approached the woman as if she was my best customer. I'd come up with a plan for her next visit after watching her walk off with a pricey candle during her last trip to the store, but I couldn't prove it.

"Mrs. Simms, how are you today?"

"Fine, fine," she muttered, and I could smell the liquor on her breath. It was hard to tell how long she'd been at it, but I imagined it had started well before lunch.

"So what can I help you with today?"

She looked around, then said, "I'm just browsing. Go ahead, do whatever you need to do."

"Nonsense, my first priority is each and every customer. Now we have some specials today. Let me show you." I took her arm and dragged her from spot to spot, making up odd specials that would have driven Eve insane if she'd been there to hear them.

Mrs. Simms was obviously uncomfortable with my close presence, since it meant she wasn't free to stuff something under her coat. I gave her ten minutes to flee from the store, but it took her only seven. As she started to bolt, I said, "Mrs. Simms, I feel guilty for deserting you in the past, but those days are over. Whenever you come back to At Wick's End, and I mean whenever, I will be right by your side, helping you pick out just the perfect thing, no matter how many other customers are in the shop. I will be right there, do you understand?"

She muttered something as she broke for the door. I doubted she'd be back, not with all my "special attention," but if she did venture in my door again, I was bound and determined that she wouldn't leave with a single thing she hadn't paid for.

Things were quiet for most of the afternoon, and I was glad we were just open till five. I knew Erin's shop didn't close until six, so if I hurried preparing my deposit, I could drop it off at the bank and still have half an hour on the water. I was eager to get back to it. Seeing the proprietress wouldn't hurt, either.

At two minutes before five, I bolted the door to At Wick's End and headed for the bank.

Erin was totaling out her own register when I got there fifteen minutes later. "You're closing early, too?" I asked, failing to hide the disappointment in my voice.

She smiled. "Don't look so grim. I decided it was a slow day, and to be honest with you, I thought making those candles might be fun. You can still take a kayak out if you'd like."

"Are you sure you wouldn't like a quick lesson in candlemaking first?"

"That's all you need, teaching candlemaking on your time off."

"Hey, I'm happy to do it. I really enjoy making them."

She shook her head. "You go grab a kayak and I'll muddle through on my own."

I grabbed a paddle, then asked, "Are you sure? I really don't mind."

"Go," she said, adding a smile to the command.

Erin didn't have to tell me twice. I untied the kayak nearest to me and a minute later I was gliding through the water. It really was a glorious time to be out. I had that stretch of the river to myself, if I didn't count the ducks and fish. The opposite bank of the river rose up straight into the mountains, and the patchwork of autumn leaves still clinging to the trees made the reflections shimmer and glow with color. It was stunning, and I found myself wishing I'd brought my camera to capture it. I paddled around, fully enjoying myself when I happened to glance at my watch. It was quarter after six! I'd made Erin stay after work, something I knew she hated. Paddling fiercely back to her dock, I made it in four minutes and noticed that all the other boats had been pulled up onto the dock and chained down.

I lifted the kayak out and headed for her office at a dead run.

"I'm so sorry I'm late," I said as I burst in. "I got lost in my thoughts."

She was frowning over one of the lumpiest rolled candles I'd ever seen in my life. Beside it were two more, each worse than the one before. She didn't even glance at the clock. "Okay, I admit it, it's harder than it looks."

"Do you mind some advice?" I asked as I stored the paddle in its rack.

"I don't have much choice, do I?"

I picked up the candle closest to me and said, "It looks like the wax was a little stiff when you started rolling. That's not your fault at all. You don't happen to have a hairdryer around here, do you?"

"Are you kidding? I can't go a week without someone tipping over and getting drenched." She retrieved one from the bathroom as I rolled her effort back out. The sheet kept a concave shape and refused to flatten, but the wax itself was intact, so I figured it would be fine. I ran the blow-dryer over the wax and stopped as it relaxed into a flat sheet. Taking her wax, I pinched the leading edge over the wick and was satisfied with the way it rolled as I started it.

"Try it now," I told her, and watched carefully as she finished rolling the candle. It was too loose to burn very well, but it was an absolute improvement over what she'd done before.

"Look, it's perfect," she said.

"Not quite. Now let's try it again. This time, try to roll it as tightly as you can. The better you do, the longer it will burn."

"But I can't just mess it up. It's so pretty."

"Keep it if you want to, but I wouldn't burn it." I reached for one of her other efforts and started the process over again. She watched raptly, and refused when I offered her another try. "You do it. Let me learn at the feet of the master."

"I'm hardly that," I said as I quickly pinched the wick into the softened wax and rolled a tight candle.

She took it when I offered my effort and compared it to her own. "Okay, I see what you mean. I'll practice more."

"That's all it takes," I agreed.

"I wouldn't say that. I think you've got the knack, Harrison. Did you have a nice time on the river?"

"It was glorious. The leaves are beautiful, aren't they?"

"Absolutely." She looked at the clock over her desk and said, "Is that the time? I'm late. Sorry, Harrison, but I've got to go."

"Do you have a date?" I asked casually.

As she shooed me out the front door, she said, "That is none of your business, sir." To take the edge off her words, she added, "Thanks for the lesson."

"Thanks for the row. I'll be back."

"I'm counting on it."

As I headed back to River's Edge, I found myself wondering who Erin was meeting. It was frankly none of my business, she'd made that clear enough on more than one occasion, but there was a part of me that wished she'd been rushing around to meet me.

PEARLY WAS JUST finishing up mounting the last security light when I drove back to River's Edge.

I said, "They look good."

"If you don't mind the irony that we're putting them up a day late, I suppose you're right."

"Do think this is a waste?" The bill for the lights was pretty healthy, but I didn't feel I'd had any choice.

"No, Harrison, don't pay any attention to me. I'm in a dark mood, and I'm not afraid to admit it to the world. The only company I'm fit for tonight is my own."

"I'll leave you to it, then," I said as I excused myself.

"Now don't go off like that. I wasn't talking about you. It's the finer gender I'm discussing."

"If you have problems with the woman in your life, I'm the last one to discuss it with. I'm going through a bit of a dry spell myself."

"Dry spell? Don't I wish. I happen to be in the awkward position of having three different women vying for my attention at the moment."

"Why Pearly, I never would have taken you for a ladies' man." I hated to admit it, but I was enjoying some of the man's discomfort.

"Laugh if you will, but it's serious enough. Harrison, since my dear sweet wife died, I haven't been involved with anyone. The hole where she isn't is still entirely too large. I believed, in my naïveté, that if I dated several ladies at the same time, I wouldn't be confronted with any one of them getting too close. I wasn't necessarily trying to keep secret the fact that I was seeing them all, but confound it, they somehow managed to find out about one another anyway, and now they've given me an ultimatum. I'm to choose one or lose all three."

I patted him on the shoulder. "Pearly, I wish you the best, but I wouldn't trade places with you for anything in the world."

"I'd say you're a wise man for that decision alone, Harrison. Well, I'm finished here. What say we give them a test?"

"What do I do?" It was nearly dark, with the hours of sunlight lessening with each passing day.

"Stand here in the shadows and we'll check them. Let me throw the breaker first."

He came back a minute later, and I said, "Sorry, it didn't work." It was as dark as when he'd left.

"Ah, watch this." He stepped off the porch and the lights suddenly came on in all their intensity, nearly blinding me.

"They work on motion sensors," he explained. "That should scare off any would-be vandals, don't you think?"

"It should do the trick. I know it will certainly get my attention upstairs."

"The perils of living at the establishment you own," Pearly said as he put his tools away. "We each have our own problems, and I trust we haven't been given more than we can handle."

"I hope you're right."

I left him to his own dilemma and headed upstairs to my apartment. It had been a long day, and though the kayaking had been an even bigger treat than before, I was feeling the strain of that last sprint in my shoulders and arms. A quiet night was what I needed and hoped beyond reasonable expectation that I would have one.

I WAS JARRED awake in the middle of the night by a horrific shrieking. It took me a few precious seconds to realize it was coming from a smoke alarm outside my apartment.

Stumbling into a pair of sweats and a T-shirt, I put on my bear slippers, a present I'd received from an ex-girlfriend, and rushed out into the hall. I'd expected the place to be full of smoke, but there were just a few wisps of it coming up the stairs. The candleshop! A fire would burn for weeks with all the wick and wax there. The place was an absolute haven for combustibles.

At least I was the only full-time tenant in the building.

Then I remembered that Markum's late hours nearly made him one, and before I headed downstairs, I rushed to his office. It was dark inside and the door was locked. Short of breaking the door down, I had no choice. Chances are he was off on one of his salvage missions. At least I hoped so.

I found the reason for the screaming alarm at the bottom of the stairs. Someone had taken one of the outside trash-cans and put it at the foot of the door. The fire had almost burned itself out in the can, but the smell was absolutely awful. I started to drag the can outside so I could hose it off, but the heat from it was too much.

First things first. I reached up and reset the smoke alarm, and was rewarded by sudden, blissful silence. I was suddenly glad Belle had invested in loud ones, though my ears would probably be ringing for weeks. I debated climbing back upstairs for a hot-pad to drag the trashcan away, but it was late, I was tired and in a foul mood. Someone was messing with me, and I didn't like it one bit. There hadn't been enough trash in the can to catch the walls on fire. It was a nuisance prank, no more and no less. I pulled off my shirt, wrapped it around my hand three or four times, then grabbed the handle and pulled the can outside. There was a hose nearby, tucked away in a stylish, little planter Pearly had built, so I turned the water on and heard a satisfying sizzle as the stream hit the remaining embers.

At least the security lights worked. The second I moved for the hose, the place lit up like a used car lot. So why hadn't I noticed it before, when the culprit had been there lighting the fire? So much for my early-warning system. I'd no doubt slept right through the earlier lighting. It had taken a full-scale alarm to rouse me from my sleep.

As I started to put the hose back up, I glanced at Heather's front door. The sign announcing her moving sale was gone. In its place was one that said, BACK IN TWO WEEKS. When had she changed it? Was it related to the fire in the stairwell? I knew Heather was upset when I'd leased

Sanora the pottery space, but I couldn't see her doing such a childish thing as dragging a trashcan into my building and setting it on fire. Still, she'd been acting strangely lately. I wished she'd talk to me and stop running away.

But there was nothing I could do about it until the next time I saw her.

I pulled the trashcan, now cool to the touch, to the back of River's Edge, but kept it away from the building, just in case, though there was more water than ash in the can at the moment.

I walked back into the building headed for my apartment when the smell hit me. Though the fire had been a minor inconvenience, the odor of burned rubbish was a genuine problem. I propped open the front door downstairs, then opened the two windows at the top of the landing upstairs, hoping for a cross breeze that would get rid of the smell. I sniffed at my clothes, and sure enough, they reeked of smoke. I jerked off my clothes and buried them in my hamper, then got into the shower and scrubbed until I was sure the smell was gone.

Unfortunately, I was as awake as could be, and I had three hours before the world around me came alive.

That was one benefit of owning my own business. It was never too early to go into work.

Ten

I'D been studying a dip-cut-curl candlemaking technique from one of my books, so I decided that would be the perfect distraction. There was no way I considered myself accomplished enough to actually pull it off, but it was an intriguing process, and I looked forward to tackling it. I was surprised by how the time flew. Millie opened at 6:00 A.M., and I'd planned to be there when she unlocked her door, but it was half past the hour when I realized how long I'd been working.

She met me with a grim expression as I walked in. She said, "So you heard the news."

"Heard it? I'm the one who put it out. How did you find out, though? I didn't think anybody else knew."

Millie said, "What are you talking about?"

"The fire in the stairwell. It was just a prank, but it nearly scared me to death. How did you hear about it?"

Millie said, "Let's back up and start over. Did you hear someone tried to run Sanora over this morning?"

"Tell me what happened."

Millie explained, "Vera Quimby called me early this morning. She's got a fondness for her police scanner, don't ask me why. She says it soothes her to have voices in her apartment. So she jolts awake when she hears Sanora's name being broadcast to the dispatcher, and naturally she felt the need to call me and wake me up. George was not a happy camper when that happened, until I filled him in. You know he volunteers with the rescue squad, so he made a few calls for me and it turns out Sanora's okay. She was jogging two hours ago on Hickory Lane and some nit in a Wee Haul rental truck forced her into the bushes. She's got some cuts and scratches from the fall, but other than that, she's fine. The thing is, Sanora claims it was deliberate."

"I can't believe it. It's kind of a conspicuous weapon, isn't it?"

Millie shook her head. "Harrison Black, it's serious business, if it's true. Now you know I'm no fan of Sanora Gaston's, but that doesn't mean I wish ill of her either. The sheriff's tracking down rentals in the area, and you'll never believe who's name popped up on the list."

"I couldn't even guess," I said.

"George heard this through the grapevine, so it's reliable enough, though I'm having trouble swallowing it."

"Who was it?" I pressed.

"Our very own Heather Bane. Now is that an odd coincidence or not? Of course I doubt it was her. Last I heard, she was in Charlotte staying with a friend."

I knew better. After all, she'd been in town sometime the night before to change that sign on her door. Could she have rented the van to move some of her stock? Had she planned to run Sanora down, or was it an accident too good to pass up when she'd seen her rival jogging alone down a dark, deserted road? No, I couldn't believe any of it, no matter how logical it sounded. But did I owe it to Sheriff Morton to tell him that Heather had every reason to be driving that van, and a few motives of her own to send Sanora off into the bushes?

"You're awfully quiet, Harrison. You know something."

I shrugged. "It's a terrible thing, isn't it? I'd love a cup of coffee and one of those blueberry muffins, if you have any."

She wasn't buying it, not for a second. "I'm not serving you until you come clean. What is it?"

I should have known better than to try to keep something from Millie. She was the eyes, the ears, and in some ways the heart of River's Edge. "Do you have a second?"

"For you, I'll manage it." She called out, "Vera, I'm stepping out a moment. Would you watch the front?"

"Be right there," Mrs. Quimby called out, and she was as good as her word. "Harrison, did you hear the news?"

"I already told him," Millie said, and I watched Mrs. Quimby deflate. "We'll be back in a shake."

I led Millie to Heather's storefront and pointed to the window. "The sign changed sometime from nine last night to three this morning. Heather was in town, and we both know she had reason enough to hate Sanora."

Millie shook her head, a frown creasing her lips. "I don't believe it. Not from Heather."

"You sound certain," I said.

"You would be, too, if you knew that girl as well as I do. She wouldn't do it, Harrison."

"I want to believe that myself, but we can't go by what's in our hearts and not our heads. We should tell the sheriff about this."

"And give him more rope to hang Heather? I don't think so. He's the great detective, let him figure it out for himself. I won't be a party to locking her up."

"I don't know," I said hesitantly. "It could be important."

"Let me track Heather down and speak with her before you say anything, Harrison. Give me a day, that's all I'm asking. What could a day hurt?"

I wanted to say it could mean the difference between attempted murder and a successful one, but I had to go with Millie's instincts. After all, chances were Morton would ignore my input anyway.

"You've got one day. Then I tell him," I said.

Millie smiled gently. "If I can't resolve this in a day, I'll tell the sheriff myself. Now let's go get you that muffin. And Harrison, why don't you keep your observation to yourself? I'm happy to have Vera working for me, but she has a tendency to talk out of turn."

"Okay by me," I said, relieved to have the burden lifted, if only for a day. Chances were Millie was right and there was a reasonable explanation for what had happened. I just couldn't imagine what it could be.

AS I STARTED for At Wick's End, Sanora Gaston called out to me. "Harrison, do you have a minute?"

"Absolutely. Hey, I'm glad you're all right. Do you want to grab a cup of coffee?"

She shook her head. "I'm not in the mood to face Millie this early. Come down to the shop."

I followed her to The Pot Shop, and she locked the door behind us. "I don't want anybody trying to get a sneak-peek of my grand opening."

"You're still going through with it after what happened this morning?" I asked.

"Absolutely. Why shouldn't I?" She studied me a moment, then added, "So you've heard?"

"Everybody in Micah's Ridge has probably heard by now. I can't believe you're still going to open today."

"Harrison, this thing is getting blown way out of proportion. The more I think about it, I'm sure it wasn't intentional. After all, who would want to hurt me?"

"Tell me what happened."

She paced around the room, straightening things now

and then as she spoke. "I was jogging along, just as I do every morning, and I looked up as a truck approached. It was a big red Wee Haul, so I moved a little more to the edge to give them plenty of room to get around me. The next thing I know, the truck's drifting toward me. I jumped into the bushes and barely missed falling over the side of the road into the river."

I said, "And you don't think it was meant for you?"

She laughed softly. "Come on. Who in their right mind would use a big red truck for a hit and run? You've got to be joking."

I pointed to her arms, where she had bandages showing and hints of yellow beneath them. "That doesn't look like a joke to me."

"Whoever was driving probably didn't even see me. No doubt they were studying a map when they should have been watching the road."

"So why did you call it in?" I pressed.

Sanora looked uncomfortable with the question. "Okay, since Aaron died I've been a little jumpy. I overreacted, I admit it."

"You should still be more careful," I said.

"Yes, sir," she said with a slight grin.

"So is that why you asked me down here?"

Sanora said sheepishly, "Actually, I was wondering if you'd do the honors and cut the grand-reopening ribbon."

"I thought the mayor was doing that for you." I'd heard Sanora had pulled about every string she had to get the mayor to come.

"She was supposed to, but I got a call this morning. She's delivering twins and it could take her all day." Since Micah's Ridge was too small to have a full-time mayor running things, Katherine Drake presided over things when her medical practice allowed it. Her rival for office, and our deputy mayor, Catherine Green, normally stepped in, but she wasn't fond of public appearances, most likely one of the reasons she kept coming in second in our mayoral races. The last campaign had been filled with signs that sported giant Cs and Ks, and for a while Micah's Ridge looked like an episode of *Sesame Street* run amok.

"Sure, why not," I said. After all, how bad could it be? Say a few words, cut a giant ribbon, and get on with my day. "What time do you need me?"

"The press is coming around one," she said. "Thanks, Harrison, you're a lifesaver."

"My pleasure. Now if you'll excuse me, I've got some candles to make before I open At Wick's End."

"See you around one," Sanora said as she let me out.

"I'll be there."

I'd been hoping to get a little practice in before I had to open the candleshop, but I was stunned to find Mrs. Jorgenson's monstrous car idling in front of At Wick's End, though it was a good five minutes before we were scheduled to open. Eve was already inside. She'd turned on all the lights, and I could look through the window and see her busily restocking the shelves, something I should have already taken care of myself. No doubt I would hear about it from my lone employee, but I resisted the urge to dash in and help her.

I approached Mrs. Jorgenson's car and before I could get within ten feet of it, she threw the door open and stepped out.

"Good morning," I said in my most level voice.

"Now before you say anything, I know I'm early for our next lesson."

"By a day at least," I said, trying to hide my chagrin with a smile. I needed more practice before I was ready to tackle anything new with her. After all, I was barely half a step ahead of her when it came to our candlemaking lessons, no matter how much I practiced and studied on my off-hours. There was only so much time I could devote to actual candlemaking, as much as I enjoyed it. I needed time to get away from the wax and the wicks, so I could bring a fresh attitude to it every time I worked. Kayaking on the Gunpowder River was just the kind of diversion I needed, but it was getting inconvenient having to trot down to Erin's every time I wanted to go for a paddle.

Mrs. Jorgenson looked apologetic, something I wished I could get on film. "I simply can't wait. If a lesson right now inconveniences you, I'm more than willing to pay extra for the privilege."

"No, ma'am, I won't take advantage of you like that. Come on in; I'll set things up for a lesson."

As she followed me inside, Eve said, "You're late," the last word dying on her lips as she saw Mrs. Jorgenson following close behind me.

"Look who I found in the parking lot waiting for us to open."

I swear Eve almost curtseyed. "I didn't see you there. I would have opened early if I'd only realized."

Mrs. Jorgenson said, "No need to apologize, dear, I wasn't expected today. I trust you can run things while Harrison gives me a lesson?"

"Of course," Eve stammered.

"Very well. Harrison?" She called out to me as she headed for our classroom in back of the store.

"I'm right behind you," I said as I offered Eve a broad wink.

In the classroom area, I said, "I need to start the wax melting. Do you mind if we use pellets today, since you already know how to chip off the block?"

I didn't think there was a chance in the world she'd agree with it, but to my surprise she said, "That would be fine. They melt quite a bit faster, don't they? Besides, I have the wax-pounding down to an art."

As I set up two stations for melting, she said, "Are you going to be dipping with me today?"

I nodded as I turned on the burners and started the water boiling. "We're going to be doing flats and braids today, so we'll need some freshly dipped tapers to start with."

After the water started boiling, I poured the wax beads into the double boilers and got the wicks ready. Mrs. Jorgenson watched the process, then asked, "Did you know Mr. Gaston well?"

"Not really," I said idly, watching the wax start to melt.

She pressed on though. "I understand foul play may have been involved."

That got my attention. I looked up from the wax and said, "As far as the sheriff is concerned, it was accidental. Why do you ask?"

Was she actually blushing? No, it had to be the light in the classroom. After a moment, she said, "Normally I don't speculate on idle gossip, but I heard from my gardener that there was some doubt about the circumstances. Being on the scene and all, I thought you might be aware of more than the police are privy to."

"They seem to be satisfied with their conclusions."

She looked triumphant. "Aha, you don't believe it either. Tell me, Mr. Black, who is it you suspect?"

Should I tell her, or let it slide? The last thing I wanted was for Mrs. Jorgenson to be involved in a situation Markum and I were investigating. Then I got an idea. I took a deep breath, then said, "Can I tell you something in strict and utter confidence?"

She nodded vigorously, so I said, "The electrical cord of the wheel appeared to be a little too perfectly frayed."

She nodded. "So the bucket of overturned water was prearranged as well."

"Mrs. Jorgenson, I'd appreciate it if you didn't tell anybody what I've told you." What possible excuse could I use to get her to hold her tongue? Then I had it. "We don't want any of our suspects to be forewarned. And," I added for dramatic flair, "If you say anything, you could be in danger."

Her pupils dilated and she took a quick sharp breath of air. "Of course. I understand completely. You will keep me informed though, won't you?"

"I promise," I said. "Now why don't we dip some candles and see what we can come up with today?"

She forgot about Aaron Gaston quickly enough once we were dipping candles, and I only hoped she'd keep her focus on wax and not homicide.

Once we both had suitable tapers in translucent wax, I hung them on the cooling rack. We had eight tapers between us, plenty for experimenting.

Mrs. Jorgenson asked, "What happens now? Shouldn't we twist them or something?"

I said, "We have to let the wax cool a little." I retrieved two rolling pins, matching pieces of maple, then touched the surface of one of our candles. It felt solid, not tacky at all. Snipping the candles' connected wick, I took one and handed the other to my student.

"Now the first step is to roll the candle with the pin to flatten it. Not all the way," I said as she started from the very top. "Leave about an inch at the top and bottom."

"Why not flatten it the entire length?" she asked.

"The bottom needs to be round so it can still fit into a base. As for the top, I just think it looks better that way."

I looked up from my worked candle and saw that she'd merely managed to somehow square up a round candle. "You're going to have to press harder than that," I said. "Flatten it out to around three eighths of an inch thick."

She put more effort into it and soon had the desired thickness.

"Now what?" she asked.

I picked my own flattened candle up and said, "Start twisting it with your hands like this." I twisted and kneaded the wax until I had a fairly true taper. I'd done it several times before, so it had become a practiced skill. Mrs. Jorgenson's attempt turned out rather differently. Her taper had a definite cant to the left, while the spiral itself was an undulating wave of wax. She held it toward me, both of us studying her efforts critically, then thrust it into my hands. "Fix it and show me what I did wrong."

I took the taper from her, worked at the wax more until I had a fairly uniform taper, then straightened the whole thing into a decent spiral.

"I believe I see now. Let's try it again."

As I severed the wick between two more tapers, she said, "Do mind if you supervise me instead of twisting your own candle? I really could use the guidance."

"Of course," I said as I laid the taper in my hand aside. I resented the command for a moment, then remembered how much I was charging her for this private lesson.

"Harder, that's it, really roll it out," I instructed as she worked.

After we were both satisfied with her efforts, I said, "Now it's time to pull back a little. You aren't trying to get the twist in a single motion. Don't be afraid to work with the wax."

Her second effort was a little better than the first, but only by a little. I'd planned to get into braiding with her in the same lesson, but it was not to be. We'd have to postpone that to another session. If there was one thing I'd learned about Mrs. Jorgenson since we'd started our lessons, it was that she demanded she master each and every task before going onto the next phase.

I dipped some of the reserve tapers into warm water.

"Why on earth did you do that? I'm not finished with them," she said fiercely. Mrs. Jorgenson hated it when she didn't master a technique on the first or second attempt.

"We need to keep the wax warm. We could use an oven just as easily, or even dip them a dozen more times, but this should work best for what we're doing."

"If you say so," she said.

By the time she'd gone through all the candles we'd dipped, her technique was just starting to come around to something resembling my first effort. It was gratifying that there was at least one form of candlemaking I'd mastered quicker than she had, but this was certainly no time to gloat about it. I said, "If you'd like to try your hand at braiding candles, we can have another lesson right now."

She scowled. "I need to master this one first. I'll be back, don't you worry about that," Mrs. Jorgenson said. Out in the main part of the store again, she said, "I believe I'll take some of those wax beads. They are rather convenient."

"Yes, ma'am. Anything else I can get you?"

She thought about it a moment, then said, "Let's have a few more spools of wick, and I need six of your beeswax kits." We'd tackled rolling candles out of sheets of wax earlier.

"Brushing up, are you?"

Mrs. Jorgenson sniffed the air. "These are for my grand-children. They spend entirely too much time on their computers, and these kits should do nicely to distract them from their monitors."

"That's a wonderful idea."

As I totaled her bill and had her sign the receipt, I said, "Do you want to go ahead and schedule the next session, or should we just play it by ear again?"

She wasn't amused, not in the least. "Make it in three days. I'll have mastered the twists by then."

"There's no doubt in my mind," I said as I helped carry her purchases out to her car. After every previous lesson, she'd taken her efforts proudly home with her, but I no-ticed I'd forgotten them.

I said, "Give me a second and I'll go get your candles."

"That won't be necessary," she said. "By tomorrow I'll have much better tapers."

"Good for you," I said as I stepped away from the car.

She seemed to think about it for a few seconds, then said, "I don't suppose it would hurt anything to take them with me. Would you mind?"

"Not at all," I said, glad she hadn't abandoned her efforts.

Eve met me at the door. "She forgot these," she said, nearly out of breath as she pushed a bag into my hands. The tapers were all safely wrapped and in the bag.

"Thanks, Eve."

I passed them on to Mrs. Jorgenson, and she grabbed my hand before I could release it. "About Mr. Gaston," she said in a lowered voice. "Do keep me informed."

"As soon as I know anything," I said.

She nodded and drove away, and I watched until she disappeared. I wasn't sure about this new development, having the richest woman in Micah's Ridge butting into a murder investigation. It could lead to a lot of trouble, for all concerned.

But I couldn't waste too much time worrying about it, either.

I had a business to run, a complex to watch over, and if time permitted, a murder to solve.

Eleven

"**WELCOME** to the grand reopening of The Pot Shot," I said to the crowd of onlookers poised in front of Sanora's pottery shop. I had no idea how she'd drummed up so many people on such short notice, but I was impressed. Not only were there nearly a hundred people in the audience, there was a reporter from *The Gunpowder Report,* our local newspaper, and a camera crew from KRZY, our local television affiliate.

If this was her basic, spur-of-the-moment promotion work, I couldn't imagine what a well-thought-out campaign must look like. I doubted I'd be able to get this kind of a turnout unless I started giving candles away. Maybe not even then.

I looked down at my notes, then said, "River's Edge welcomes you. Feel free to shop all of our fine stores while you're here." I'd suggested the last bit to Sanora, and she'd heartily okayed it. After all, while we did run separate businesses, we were also part of a community. Besides, I thought it wouldn't hurt her standing with the other tenants, and the fact that it might throw a little business our way at the candleshop hadn't escaped me.

But these folks were here for Sanora, and I felt obligated to give the pottery center stage.

"There are some great deals inside, there's food and drink, too, so come on in." With that, I used a giant pair of scissors to sever the red ribbon Sanora had strung across the door, and she was officially open for business.

As folks moved toward the open doors, I thought I spotted Heather in the background, but I must have been mistaken. Coming to Sanora's opening was something I just couldn't see her doing. I regretted she was missing the opportunity for sales, but shutting her store down had been her decision.

I found myself standing beside Tick after the crowd vanished into The Pot Shot.

"Nice speech, Harrison," she said. "I didn't know you were available for rallies and celebrations."

"Believe me, I have no intention of making a habit of this. Sanora needed a quick substitute when the mayor canceled, so she asked me."

"You did fine," Tick said.

"Do you think this crowd is going to wander around to our shops after they see what The Pot Shot has to offer?"

Tick said, "It's too soon to tell, but it couldn't hurt. How's business at the candleshop been lately?"

"We're keeping our heads above water," I said. "How's the world of antiques?"

"Oh, it stays pretty steady between our walk-in customers and our regulars. Why, I'm even on the Internet now, if you can believe that."

"Getting much business there?"

She shook her head. "Not particularly, though I must admit, I don't give it the time it requires. I have a young lady from the high school working my web page. It was her idea, since she had a debt to work off with me."

"How did that come about?"

Tick said, "Young Maria has a passion for Depression Glass, and we barter for her services. You haven't been in the shop lately, you should stop by. I've just gotten some lovely furniture from Ireland."

"It must be great fun amassing your stock. Do you ever go on any expeditions yourself?"

She nodded. "In fact, I was supposed to go to Scotland two weeks ago, but I had to cancel at the last minute. My traveling companion backed out on me almost as we were boarding, and it's no fun going alone."

"I understand that," I said as I started for The Pot Shot. "Are you coming?"

"Do you know, I've never stepped one foot into that pottery shop? I don't appreciate the medium at all."

"How about candles? You know you're always welcome in At Wick's End."

She shuddered visibly. "Thank you for the invitation, but no, I'm afraid not. You see, I've got a horrid fear of fire. I'm afraid I spend all my time with my treasures."

"Well then, maybe we could have lunch at Millie's sometime."

Tick frowned, then said, "I seem to keep saying no to you, don't I? I'd honestly love to, Harrison, but I don't have someone like Eve watching over my wares." She glanced at an antique watch pinned to her sweater, then said, "I'd better go back to the shop."

"I'll catch up with you later, then."

"Do visit me sometime soon," she said as she headed back to her world of antiques.

Sanora was busy behind the cash register, so I wandered around the shop. The display I'd seen earlier sporting many of Aaron's pieces had already grown smaller, and from the look of things, there wouldn't be anything left by the next day. What was it about the work of some artists and craftsmen that as soon as no new pieces would ever be available, the remaining ones sold so quickly, and in most cases for so much more? Folks had grabbed up many of Belle's creations after her death, until I held some in reserve for the shop with "Not For Sale" stickers attached. In a way, it kept her a part of the shop she'd so carefully created.

The press had left as soon as they'd gotten their pictures, but the browsers and buyers were buzzing about in full force. Sanora noticed me and waved me to her.

"Thanks again for doing that, Harrison," she said as she wrapped a tea set up in thick brown paper.

"My pleasure. If you don't need me, I'm going to head back to At Wick's End."

"See you later," she said as she ran a customer's card through her register. I noticed her sign-up sheet for classes was already filling up, and I wondered how to juice up the attendance in our candlemaking classes. Maybe a display in the front window, or even an ad in the paper. Eve had been pushing for more exposure, and I was ready to listen to her.

I moved down the wide walkway of River's Edge back toward my shop and glanced at the river beside us. The Gunpowder was flowing past at a good clip, and for a moment I wished I could be out there on it. Not today, though. I had too much work to do. Thinking of kayaking made me wonder about Erin and what her history was. Had she truly been interested in candlemaking when she'd come by the shop, or was there a chance she was interested in the candlemaker?

I laughed out loud at that. My imagination was definitely getting the better of me. April May had told me clearly enough that she knew Erin was still getting over someone, and besides, I didn't have time for someone in my life, not with the demands of my responsibilities. Still, I missed those jitters that made me feel alive. When I fall for a woman, I tend to fall pretty hard, and a part of me yearned for that butterfly feeling in my stomach at the sound of someone special's name. I wondered if my late Great-Aunt Belle realized just how much she'd put on my plate by leaving me River's Edge. Probably, she was a crafty old gal, and I found myself missing her every day. There were a thousand questions I would have loved to ask her, but then again, if she'd still been around I wouldn't be running At Wick's End.

I glanced in Tick's antique shop and saw there were a handful of customers in her shop. Maybe, if we were lucky, some of them would migrate all the way down to the candleshop.

I found Eve doing inventory when I walked in the door. There wasn't a customer in sight.

"How was your speech?" she asked. "Sorry I missed it, but someone had to watch the store, goodness knows it's been quiet though. Did many people show up?"

"There were about a hundred, I'd guess," I said, "And the speech was everything it needed to be: short and to the point. Have we had anyone drift in yet?"

"Not since you left. I certainly hope we get some of the traffic here. You did mention us in your speech, didn't you?"

"I mentioned everyone," I admitted, not wanting to get into my lack of a specific endorsement. I still believed I'd handled the situation correctly, but I had no desire to get into that particular discussion with Eve.

I glanced at the clock. "You can leave early again today, if you'd like. I should be able to handle things here."

"There's nowhere I need to be," she said. Funny, just last week she'd skipped out early nearly every single day. Something had changed in her life, there was no doubt about that.

I bit my lower lip, then asked, "Eve, is there anything you want to talk about? On a personal level? I've been told I'm a good listener."

"There's certainly no need for that," she said abruptly.

"If you change your mind," I said, "I'm here."

Eve ruffled the papers in her hands, then said, "I've got work to do." She disappeared into the storeroom and I regretted saying anything to her. When would I learn? While she and Belle had been great friends, I still got the impression that Eve barely tolerated me.

A few customers managed to find their way down to At Wick's End, but they were more interested in browsing than buying. When it was time to close out the register for the day, I realized we were actually quite a bit below our normal daily take. So much for the trickle-down theory of customers shopping all the stores at River's Edge. I sent Eve home and closed out the books, filled out the deposit, and locked the shop up for the evening. It was one of our early closing days, and I was looking forward to a little time away from River's Edge. If I hurried, I might be able to get down to Erin's boating shop before she closed. But the bank deposit came first.

I dropped the bag off, and made it to Erin's twenty minutes before closing. No one was there, though. I found a sign on the door that said, GONE FOR THE DAY. WHITEWATERING ON THE NOLICHUCKY.

So much for that. I wondered how much a kayak cost, and more important, if I could afford it on my limited budget. It would be nice to hit the water whenever I felt like it and not have to rely on someone else. Then again, I wouldn't have the excuse to pop in on Erin anymore either.

I'd have to think about it, then consult my bank balance.

I was in no hurry to get back to River's Edge, not after being so eager to leave it, so I decided to head over to the library to see what was new in the stacks. I had my share of mysteries on the shelves from Belle, but I also had a passion for biographies, one my late great-aunt hadn't shared with me.

Robyn, my friend and the best research librarian in the state, was busy helping a patron. I waved to her, and she acknowledged me with a bob of her head. I wandered over to the biographies, located near the open study area, and was browsing through the Gs when I heard a familiar voice.

It was Cragg, and from the look of things, he'd gotten himself into a spot of trouble.

I didn't mean to eavesdrop, but it was hard not to, given the volume of the two men's voices. Cragg was talking with a man nearly twice his size, with thick shoulders and hands that looked like they could crush rocks.

"Stay away from her," the man said, punctuating his point by jabbing Cragg's chest. The attorney stood up under the assault, though he did back up a step or two.

"Let her make up her own mind," Cragg said.

"She did. She wants me."

Cragg said, "When she tells me that, I'll believe it. That first tap was free. If you touch me again, I'll sue you until you've lost every last dime to your name."

"Lawyers. What a bunch of cowards."

Robyn suddenly appeared, and though she was quite a bit smaller than Cragg, let alone the giant with him, she marched in between them as if she was twenty feet tall.

"I've told you both twice to lower your voices. Leave this library, and I mean right now."

The big man said, "We're not finished."

Robyn walked up under his chin and said, "Believe me, you don't want to push this. Now are you going to go peacefully?"

The big man looked at her a second, then said, "Yeah, I'm going." He stopped and said to Cragg, "Leave her alone."

Cragg didn't comment, and the big man left.

Robyn was still frowning at Cragg. "You know better than that, Gary. Go on."

He looked at Robyn incredulously. "You can't be serious."

"You'd better believe I am. Go home, go somewhere

and cool off, and don't come back until you can act with some decorum."

He shook his head and walked out, going right past me in the stacks. Cragg didn't notice me, and I wasn't about to call attention to myself. I waited until he was gone, then joined Robyn.

I said, "What was that all about?"

"I'm not one of these modern apologists who believe rowdiness belongs in the stacks. Libraries are meant for reading and contemplation, not debating and fistfights."

"Wow, I never knew you were so tough," I said, fighting to hide my smile.

"I can be, when it comes to oafs and barbarians. Is there anything I can do for you?"

"I was wondering if you had any biographies on Genghis Khan. Tyrants have always fascinated me."

"If you've forgotten your alphabet again, sing your ABCs."

I smiled. "Let me see, how does that go again?"

" 'Bye, Harrison."

After she was gone, I picked out a few books and checked them out at the circulation desk. Heading back to River's Edge, I wondered who the behemoth Cragg had been arguing with was. From the sound of it, a woman was at the heart of their disagreement, and I couldn't help believing that woman was Sanora Gaston. Was it possible she was involved with that stranger? He didn't seem like he was her type, but then again, who knew for sure? Aaron had been a slight man with a willowy build. Maybe she'd been searching for a change from her ex-husband when she'd dated the man-mountain. Gary Cragg was more smitten than I'd realized if he was willing to go up against him, no doubt about that.

I wasn't about to let up on him. If he was that taken with Sanora, could he be pushed to commit murder to save his chances with her? It was hard not to let my dislike for the man creep into my judgment. Blast it all, it was almost as if I wanted him to be guilty.

My stomach rumbled as I got into my truck, and I suddenly had no taste for the spaghetti I'd planned to cook for myself. Fortunately, A Slice of Heaven was on my way home. April May was behind the counter, and the place was hopping, as usual. All the tables were full, and there were a few kids at the door waiting for one to open up. The jukebox was serenading the crowd with some jazz, and I wondered who had redeemed their pizza for Miles Davis. Whoever it was, I approved. That was April's thing. Some places gave out free pizzas; April allowed a frequent diner to choose his own record for the jukebox. But not even the music could make me feel like being part of the crowd. There were times, more and more lately, it seemed, that I didn't want much company during my time away from At Wick's End.

I studied April May as she zipped around the ovens and register, and I wondered if she ever got a break.

I asked, "Do you have a night off, April?"

She cut a pizza she'd just taken out of the oven and expertly slid it into a box. "Why Harrison, are you asking me out on a date?"

"No, that's not what I meant."

"What, you think you could do better?" she asked, and I couldn't for the life of me tell if she was being serious or not.

"To be perfectly honest with you, I have a feeling I'd be overmatched."

That brought a chuckle, and a sigh of relief from me. She said, "I've got a feeling you'd be right." She looked around me, then asked, "What happened, run out of eligible young women? Last time you were here you went through two in one evening. My friend, Micah's Ridge isn't all that big for you to be so casual about it all."

"I don't guess you'd believe me if I told you neither one was a date."

She patted my hand after she passed the boxed pizza on to its owner. "If it makes you feel any better believing that, you go right ahead."

I knew it was a hopeless battle, sparring with her like that. "April, I'd like a medium pepperoni pizza, to go."

She said, "Come on, Harrison, I didn't mean anything by it. If you want to stay, I'll find you a table."

"Honestly, I'm not much in the mood for company tonight."

She nodded. "If you want to wait outside, I'll have your pizza ready in twelve minutes."

"Sounds great. I'll be out by my truck." I slid my money across to her, and she rang up the sale. "Thanks, April."

"You're most welcome."

Outside, the night air was growing chilly, and I was happy for the chance to wear one of my rugby shirts. I'd never played, but I loved the thick cotton of the jerseys and the bright patterns of cloth. Years before, I'd stumbled across a sale at Kohl's and happened to have enough with me to buy an even half-dozen. I had enough jerseys to last me for years.

As I leaned against my truck waiting for my pizza, I watched folks come and go, happy and lost in their own little worlds. I wanted to be a part of them, but I couldn't bring myself to joining them.

April came out right on schedule. On top of the pizza box was a bottle of beer. "You looked like you could use a drink when you got home."

I reached for my wallet, but she said, "It's on the house." As she handed them over, she said, "You're just one pie away from your own song. Any ideas about what you might pick?"

"I really liked the Miles Davis you had on when I came in."

April looked around, then lowered her voice. "Don't tell anyone, but I picked that one myself. Don't get me wrong,

I know the gimmick gets me business, but some of the choices are horrendous. When things get crazy, I get in the mood for some mellow music."

"A woman after my own heart. Thanks, April."

She saluted, then said, "I'd better get back inside before they tear the place down. Good night, Harrison."

"Good night," I called out, but she was already gone.

I considered taking my pizza to the rooftop and eating it there, but if the wind up there was anything like the breeze kicking up below, it would be too cold to enjoy it. I settled for the kitchen bar in my apartment and had just popped the lid off when someone knocked at my door.

I guess it could have been worse. I could have been in the shower.

"I'll be right there," I called out as I grabbed a slice anyway and took a healthy bite before I answered the door.

Twelve

MARKUM was at the door, and I moved aside so he could come in. "Want a slice?" I asked him before taking another bite.

"No, but if you've got another beer, I wouldn't say no to that."

I grabbed a cold one from the refrigerator and handed it to him. "What's up?"

He said, "I wanted to see what the sheriff had to say about our power cord."

"I told him what I thought, but he wasn't interested."

"Typical," Markum scowled, running a hand through his thick hair.

"Give him a break," I said. "He's got the flu, along with half his department. I don't think he has all that much time for suppositions and guesswork."

"Don't tell me you've changed your mind," Markum said.

"No, it's too much of a coincidence, I agree. I'm just not sure what we can do about it."

"We look harder at Sanora, that's what I think. She had the most reason of anyone to want him dead."

I finished a bite, then said, "Did you hear about what happened this morning?"

"No, I've been sleeping all day." Before I could make a crack, he said, "I'm trying to set something up in another time zone, so it makes more sense for me to start keeping their hours." I wanted to ask Markum what kind of salvage operation he was preparing for, but the man was remarkably closemouthed about his business. "So what happened?"

"Somebody tried to run Sanora down this morning with a Wee Haul van."

"Were there any witnesses?" Markum asked.

"Just Sanora."

Markum thought about it, took another sip from his beer, then said, "So she could have made the whole thing up."

I said, "She's got the scratches from diving off the road."

"Adds evidence to her claim, from her point of view."

I shook my head. "So why was she downplaying the whole thing when I talked to her this morning? She told me she thought the driver was probably reaching for a map and the truck started to drift over toward her. It didn't sound like she was trying to set herself up as another potential victim."

Markum shrugged. "Maybe she's just being cute, or maybe she lost her nerve and decided to backpedal."

"Do you really think she killed her ex-husband?"

Markum finished his beer, then said, "Whenever I'm faced with something like this, I ask myself, who had the most to gain? Sanora gets The Pot Shot and eliminates her ex-husband as her main competition, all with one murder. It could have been too tempting for her."

"It could have been, but from what I've heard, the two of them were friends, they weren't even dating again. Besides, her shop was supposed to be doing pretty well right where it was."

"Then why was she so eager to leave that location and come here to River's Edge?"

I didn't have an answer for that. "Surely she can't be your only suspect."

"Can you think of anyone else?"

I hated to do it, but Markum needed to know about Heather if he was going to be able to help me with Aaron Gaston's death. "Heather Bane had reason enough. Aaron broke up with her so he could see Sanora again. When that blew up in his face, she was willing to take him back, but he turned her down flat. From what I've heard, Aaron was dating someone new, but I haven't been able to find out who it was yet."

Markum grinned at me. "Aren't you the fishwife, swapping tales over the clothesline."

"Nothing like that. I just listened," I said.

"Easy, my friend, I'm impressed. So young Heather should be added to our list. Where is she, by the way? I've noticed the ever-changing signs hanging in her front window."

"That's the thing. The night I found Aaron's body, Heather was outside. When she found out Aaron was dead, she threw her cat into my arms and tore off in her car."

"So you're still cat-sitting?"

"No, she came by long enough to retrieve Esmeralda, then she was gone again."

"So Heather had the opportunity, she certainly had motive enough, and anyone with a steak knife could have skinned that cord."

"You know, I've been thinking about that," I said. "I wonder if they did an autopsy."

"What are you driving at?"

"Well, if someone actually killed Aaron by dumping that water on the cord, they had to be there when it happened. Not only that, but they had to insure that the water hit the cord and puddled up around Aaron without being near it themselves. It sounds like they left an awful lot to chance."

"So you're saying the accident was staged after our friend Aaron was already dead."

I finished off my own beer, then said, "It's a possibility."

"I wonder," Markum said as he stroked his chin. "What are the odds we could get the sheriff to demand an autopsy?"

"Too late for that. The body was cremated the second it was released."

Markum asked, "And who made that particular decision?"

"Sanora did," I admitted. "Cragg told me Aaron never got around to changing his executor and heir after their split."

"So all the more reason to suspect her."

I said, "There's somebody else I haven't mentioned yet."

Markum shook his head in amazement. "Harrison, how have you managed to find the time to run your candleshop, with all this sleuthing you've been doing on the side?"

"There's a lot of downtime in retail, so I've had plenty of time to think."

"I'm not criticizing, my friend, that was sheer admiration in my voice. So who is our fourth suspect?"

"Four?" I asked. "I've only counted Sanora and Heather so far."

"Surely you're not discounting Aaron's latest love, the mysterious Ms. X? We've already seen Aaron's pattern with women and it wouldn't surprise me in the least that our potter friend cut another one loose. Perhaps his latest, or should I say last, paramour didn't take the news as graciously as Aaron had hoped."

"I never thought about that, but it's as likely as what we've got so far."

"So don't keep me in suspense, Harrison. Let's hear it all."

"Maybe it's because I don't like him. I hate to say anything unless I'm sure."

Markum said, "Come on, this is among friends. You're not broadcasting it all over the world. What's said behind your door stays here, as far as I'm concerned."

"Okay, I know I can trust you. It's Gary Cragg."

"So there *was* something to that. I always suspected as much."

"What are you talking about?"

After a long hesitation, Markum said, "I've often wondered if Belle seized on the missing money as a way of getting rid of Sanora without kicking Aaron out as well. Cragg and Sanora were getting a little too friendly, if you ask me, and I caught her leaving his office late one night just before Belle threw her out. If I saw something, as rarely as I was present on the grounds, think what you're aunt must have seen."

"So why didn't she get rid of Cragg, too?"

"Perhaps she was waiting for a reason to present itself before she died. So your theory is that Cragg thought Sanora was still interested in her ex-husband, so he decided to eliminate his competition."

"It could be, if Cragg thought it was serious." I recounted what I'd overheard at the library between Cragg and the strange man, and Markum took it all in.

"So Cragg's still interested to the point of jealousy. I'll have to think about this. It's not as simple as I once thought."

"Is anything ever that way? So what am I supposed to do in the meantime while we're considering the facts?"

Markum said, "Keep listening and keep thinking. At least we shouldn't have to worry about the murderer striking again."

"Why do you say that?"

"What reason is left, now that Aaron is gone?"

I shook my head. "We'd have to know the motive before we can say that."

Markum nodded. "You're right, of course. It might be something besides scorn that drove the killer." He yawned once, then said, "I'm not sure this latest project is worth what it's costing me in sleep. Let's meet again tomorrow night and discuss it more, if you're game."

"I've got nothing planned," I admitted reluctantly.

"You sound remorseful about it. You haven't really dated much since you came to River's Edge, have you?"

"I've been busy," I said.

"I know how much time this place takes, but surely, for your own well-being, there's time to step out now and then. I know I find time for the fairer sex, and my schedule's worse than yours."

I said, "There are a couple of prospects, but I seem to be more interested in them than they are in me."

He stood and put a meaty paw on my shoulder. "Patience, my friend. Where there's life, there's hope."

"And then there's the hopeless," I said, trying to make a joke out of it. I wasn't all that comfortable sharing my horrific dating record of late with Markum.

"And on that note, I'll leave you."

"See you tomorrow, then."

"Tomorrow it is," Markum said as I let him out.

I wrapped up what was left of the pizza and put it in the refrigerator. It would do for lunch tomorrow or a snack tomorrow night. I couldn't afford to throw it away, not on my budget. At Wick's End hadn't turned out to be a goldmine, or even a tin one, for that matter. I was a little better off than I'd been before inheriting the place, but not enough to change my standard of living much.

Still, it was good to have a place to call my own, a worthwhile business to occupy my time, and enough friends around me to keep life interesting.

Sometimes though, I found myself wishing it wasn't quite so interesting.

AT A FEW minutes past midnight, I still hadn't been able to fall asleep, though I'd been trying for the last hour or so. Tired of tossing and turning, I decided I might as well get up, since sleep was a long time from coming. Bundling up in sweats and a heavy coat, I climbed the ladder to my rooftop getaway. It was a calm night for a change, a whisper of crispness in the air and no wind coming off the river below. I had a clear view of the water from my aerie, and to the north I could see the outline of the mountains against the sky. The stars were out in all their brilliance, and I pulled my chair from under its canopy and stared up at the autumn sky. That lasted a few minutes, and then I retrieved the blanket I kept under cover, wrapped myself in its warmth, and enjoyed the view.

I'd had no intention of falling asleep, but as the sun rose in the morning, I awoke to a new day. There was a crick in my neck and a cramp in one of my calves, but I couldn't remember getting a better night's sleep. Once summer came to River's Edge, I promised myself more nights up there in the tranquility of the night.

But that would have to wait till the cool temperatures had come and gone. It took me a few minutes to work the stiffness out of my body, and I promised myself an air mattress before I attempted another campout.

After a hot shower and a bowl of oatmeal, I was ready to tackle the world again.

Locking my apartment door, a note fluttered to the floor at my feet.

It was from Markum.

"Harrison. Called away on urgent business. Watch your back."

So if anyone was going to solve Aaron Gaston's murder, it appeared that it was going to be up to me.

"GOOD MORNING," I said to Eve as I locked the door to At Wick's End behind me.

"What's so good about it?" she asked plaintively, I knew right off the bat what kind of day I was in for. Whatever had gone wrong lately in my employee's life, she wasn't shy about bringing it to work with her.

"Let's see," I said, trying to be positive despite her disposition. "It's a gorgeous day out, we both have a place to work, and we have our health."

She didn't answer, unless her scowl could be counted as one. I wasn't going to let her bring me down, though. "Listen, if you'd like to take a personal day, that's fine by me."

I thought for a second she was going to take me up on my offer, but finally she just shook her head. "No, I'll work."

"All right then, let's work."

I assigned her the stock inventory, and even let her place the order while I waited on our first customers. I'd come a long way since my Great-Aunt Belle had left me At Wick's End, and I could handle just about every customer who came into the shop, but I still needed Eve's help with some of them, especially in the areas of candlemaking I hadn't mastered yet. As Mrs. Jorgenson's lessons proceeded along, so did my own. I wasn't sure what would happen once we'd explored all we could in the current art of candlemaking, but I'd burn that taper when I came to it. We had enough techniques to explore to last us dozens of additional lessons.

By lunchtime, I'd managed to stay out of Eve's way, but it had been an extra strain for me.

I said, "I'm going to take the first lunch, if you don't mind."

She said, "That's fine with me. I've got nowhere else I need to be."

It was obvious the morning of work hadn't done anything to improve her attitude. What I needed was some fresh air and some solitude.

I jogged up the steps to my apartment and threw a sandwich together, then grabbed a soda to go with it. I was tempted to have my little picnic up on the roof, but decided to go down to the steps of River's Edge and watch the Gunpowder flow past me.

As I unwrapped my sandwich, I wished Heather hadn't fled River's Edge, for so many reasons, not the least of which were the nice lunch breaks we'd shared in the past.

Thirteen

A voice from the river called out, "Do you happen to have enough to share?"

It was Erin, in a sleek green canoe, paddling toward the steps where I sat. The water lapped three steps below, and I often wondered just how low the stairway descended.

I said, "I've got plenty, if you don't mind bologna and cheese."

"Are you kidding? I was raised on the stuff."

I put my sandwich down and helped her steady her canoe as she climbed out. "How are you going to keep it from drifting off?"

She smiled. "You don't know your own property all that well, Harrison. There are rings mounted right in the concrete of the steps."

She tied her boat up and joined me. As I handed her half my sandwich, I said, "We'll have to share the soda."

"I don't mind if you don't. It's quite a paddle up here from my place."

"Who's watching your shop?" I asked.

"I've got a dozen signs, one for just about every occasion."

"Aren't you afraid you'll miss some business?" I asked. I felt guilty closing the candleshop at night, let alone shutting down in the middle of the day.

She shook her head. "A long time ago, I had to decide who was going to run my life, my shop or me. I might not make as much money as I would if I were more dedicated, but there's no doubt in my mind I wouldn't sleep as well, either."

"Sounds like you've got a handle on it. So what brings you to River's Edge? Did you come by for another kit?"

She shook her head. "No, I believe I'll leave the candle-making to you experts."

"So why are you here? Not that I'm not happy for the company."

She looked at the water as she spoke, taking her time before she answered. "I didn't plan to come this far, but sometimes, when I'm out on the water, I get lost in my own little world. Sounds crazy, doesn't it?"

"No, I understand it. That's one of the joys of it, as far as I can tell."

She took a bite of her sandwich, then said, "You're a loner at heart, aren't you?"

"I like people well enough," I protested.

"Hey, I'm not accusing you of anything evil, I'm just asking a question. It's okay, I'd rather be out on the water alone than just about anywhere else in the world."

I finished my sandwich before she did, but then I'd spent less time talking than she had. "I'm happy enough by myself, but if there's someone I'm comfortable with, that's nice, too."

She took a sip from the bottle of soda, then said, "I used to believe that myself."

I could tell she wanted to say more, but she stood instead and said, "Thanks for lunch. I'd better be getting back."

"Back alone on the water, or back to your shop?"

She smiled at me. "Let's just say it might be a little bit of both."

She was back in the canoe and on her way when she called out, "Thanks again for lunch."

"My pleasure," I said as she paddled away.

I hadn't heard Sanora come up behind me, and I nearly fell in when she spoke. "Hey there. Take it easy, I'm not that scary, am I?"

"No, I was just lost in a thought."

"I do that all the time. I'd ask you to join me for lunch, but it looks like you've already eaten. How long have you two been dating?"

It took me a second to realize she was talking about Erin. "We're not dating. We never have been, to tell the truth."

Sanora said, "Sorry, my mistake. You just looked cozy, sitting there sharing your meal. You must have been friends a long time."

"We just met this week," I said, surprised by the truth of it. Erin and I had skipped all of that awkwardness in our first meeting. There had been a comfort level from the start.

She said, "Wow, you make friends fast."

"It's been known to happen. So how's business? It's had to have slowed down since yesterday."

"Yesterday was good," she admitted, "But I'm not doing too badly today either. Did you get many customers down your way from all the excitement?"

"Not so you'd notice," I admitted, a little too frankly. "Don't worry about At Wick's End. We're doing fine."

"That's good to hear. Listen, there's something I wanted to ask you about."

"Fire away," I said as I drained the last of my drink.

"I found this in my office last night. It had rolled under the desk. Do you have any idea where it came from?" She held up a shiny, polished piece of quartz, and I plucked it out of her hand. I studied the facets a moment, then turned it over and found that there was a hole drilled in one end of it. It looked like something Heather would sell, most likely for a bracelet or necklace.

"I'm not sure," I said, offering it back to her.

She declined. "I've got no use for it. Maybe you can figure out who it belongs to."

I tucked it in my pocket as I saw Pearly bustling toward At Wick's End. I considered calling out to him, but from the look of his walk and the intent purpose in his stride, he probably wouldn't hear me.

Sanora asked, "I don't mean to rush you, but have you decided if you're going to extend my lease or not? If you let it lapse, I'm going to have to take out an option on my old space."

"Was it expensive to give it up?" I asked.

She misunderstood. "I'm not poor-mouthing you, Harrison, I do pretty well at my shop, no matter where it is, but I like River's Edge. It's got a lot of heart."

"I think so myself," I said.

"So have you? Decided, I mean?"

I shook my head. "It's too early to say yet, I'm sorry. I have to give things around here a chance to settle down before I decide."

"You're talking about Heather, aren't you? Listen, I'm truly sorry about all that. I didn't mean to run her off."

"I'm not so sure you did," I said. "She has a new sign up in her window now that says she'll be back in a couple of weeks."

"But I thought . . . never mind. That's good, then."

"What were you going to say?" I pressed.

"Tick told me she was gone for good. I guess she was wrong."

"For that we'll have to wait and see. Listen, I'd love to stay and chat, but I've got to get back to the shop."

"They're worse than toddlers, aren't they? I shouldn't leave mine long either."

I walked my way and she walked hers. Sanora was an enigma, no doubt about that.

Pearly Gray nearly ran me down coming out as I started to open the door to At Wick's End.

"Were you looking for me?" I asked as I stepped aside.

"No, nothing like that," he mumbled. "I'll speak with you later."

Then he was gone.

Eve's cheeks were bright crimson and there was a glistening in her eyes.

Then it hit me. She'd been having problems with her love life, and Pearly had mentioned that some of the women he'd been dating were ganging up on him. I'd never dreamed Eve was one of the women he'd been talking about. From the look of things, that particular chapter in both of their lives was written and closed.

"You can take your lunch now," I said, trying to ignore the state of agitation she was in.

"I brought mine with me. I'll just eat it in back." There was a new firm resolve in her voice and the sullenness was gone. If having it out with Pearly was what it took to make my life more tranquil, then I felt sorry for my handyman, but he'd brought it all on himself.

I just wanted a little harmony at the candleshop, and maybe I was about to get it.

That particular theory proved to be true. Eve was back to her old self again, never all that cordial before, but certainly never that snappy either.

It was as close to civility as she'd managed in a long time, and I almost felt myself blushing from her ambivalence.

I was in such a good mood that I sent Eve home half an hour before we were set to close, and to my amazement, she took me up on my offer.

A man came in three minutes before closing. He was dressed in a three-piece suit and wore a faded rose in the buttonhole, as if he'd attended a wedding a few days before and had forgotten to remove the spent flower.

"May I help you with something?" I asked.

"No, just browsing."

"I'm closing soon," I said.

"Fine. I won't be long."

He took his time, stopping at every display, picking up a few things, checking prices, then putting them down again. I felt like giving him a countdown as every thirty seconds passed, but I resisted the temptation, as hard as it was to ignore. Last-second shoppers always drove me crazy, and I was working on my patience, without sterling results.

The second-hand of the clock crawled as if through Jell-O before it finally reached closing time. "Sorry, but we're closing."

"Don't mind me," he said.

Now what could that mean? Was I going to have to throw him out physically? No one had ever failed to take the hint before, but this man was clearly not getting it.

I had a few things to take care of, and I could do them in plain sight, so I decided to let him browse. At seven minutes past, I'd done everything but close out the register.

I joined him near the back of the store near two huge, gaudy candles that Belle must have made. They were frankly not my great aunt's best work, and I'd been meaning to move them back into storage where I might finally quit tripping over them. I wasn't sure where the mold had come from for them, but Belle hadn't left them alone at that. The candles had been gilded and painted and decorated until I doubted there was a technique she hadn't tried on them.

"Interesting," the man said. "Are they for sale individually, or are they a matched set?"

I was ready to give them away just so I wouldn't have to

dust them anymore, but I'd been in business long enough to hear the avarice in the man's voice. "Oh, I couldn't think of letting one go without the other."

"How much would they be, then?"

That was a question I wasn't prepared to answer. As I wondered how much I should ask, he said, "Oh, here's the price right here."

Even with all the times I'd looked at the ugly twins, I'd missed the price tag hidden among the finery of flowing ribbons and dripping shells.

I gulped when I saw the price and was ready to discount them on the spot when he said, "I'll take them."

"That will be fine," I managed to say as I took his credit card.

As I rang the sale up, he stroked one and said, "Rather hideous, aren't they?" Realizing his words could offend, he quickly amended, "To me, at any rate. Beauty in the eye of the beholder and all that, eh?"

"They aren't my favorites of what we sell," I admitted. "But I'm curious, if you don't like them, why are you buying them?"

He studied me a second, then said, "My ex-wife is getting remarried in three days, and she had the nerve to invite me to the festivities." He took a breath, then said, "In fact, she asked me to give her away!"

"And you agreed?" I asked, honestly curious.

"I am, sir, a gentleman above all else. It was a request I couldn't refuse, in good conscience, but it's been troubling me ever since. Give her away? I never wanted her to leave in the first place. But she was intent on going, and there was nothing I could do about it. I honestly thought she'd come back to me. How wrong I was."

"I'm sorry, this must be really painful for you."

He waved a hand in the air. "I'm beyond numb with it, sir."

I had to ask, "So where do the candles come in?"

He smiled gently. "My wife loves the simple line and form. She eschews all ornamentation in her life, and sir, if ever there was something full of unnatural augmentation, this pair is gloriously it. What a wonderful wedding present these will make."

I helped him carry them out to his car, a black Buick from another era with enough real metal in it to hold magnets. We buckled the candles into the backseat and he left, whistling as he drove away.

The cash register report looked quite a bit healthier after his augmentation, and there was no doubt his purchase had made him feel better.

I tucked the deposit under my arm and locked At Wick's End whistling a tune myself.

There was a light on at Tick's antiques shop, and I glanced in to see her slumped over a chair inverted on one of her tables. I rushed inside to see if she was all right when she said, "Who's there? Harrison, what a pleasant surprise."

"Are you all right?" I asked breathlessly.

"What? Of course I am."

"When I saw you slumped over the chair, I thought . . ."

"I'm trying to repair the bloody thing and sometimes there's no clamp in the world nearly as good as a pair of human hands. Thank goodness it's quick-setting glue. I'll be with you in a minute. Feel free to look around."

I hadn't spent much time in the antique shop, but that was true of several of the businesses at River's Edge. There was so much time taken by my own shop, I didn't have many opportunities to visit with my tenants. As I let my gaze wander through the store, it amazed me Tick could find anything here. Desks were crowded with lamps and trinkets, while chairs were tucked in among bureaus and pie safes. I let my fingers trail across the stained glass of a Tiffany lamp when Tick came up beside me and told me how much it was.

I quickly pulled my hand away.

She said, "It's all right to touch it, Harrison."

"If I broke it, I'd have to work six months to replace it," I said.

She laughed. "Surely not. I'd give you a merchant's discount if that happened, but most likely I'd be able to fix it myself."

"Is that standard, you repairing your wares? Somehow it doesn't seem all that kosher."

Tick shook her head. "Spoken like a man who deals only with new stock. If I didn't add the bit of glue and screw to many of these pieces, they'd break before my customers got them home. I'm faithful to the original builder whenever I can be, and I'm happy to point out my repairs whenever I'm asked."

"I didn't mean anything by it," I said. "It's just so different from what I do."

"That's why there are markets for us both. Don't let it trouble you. I have a rather profitable side business repairing and restoring pieces I never sold in the first place. It's quite fun, actually, making something whole again. I do everything from woodworking to stained glass work. I rewire old lamps and restore chandeliers. Now what could be more fascinating than that?"

"Yes, I can see that it might be. Well, as long as you're all right, I've got to get to the bank."

"I'm afraid I've got hours to go yet before I'm ready to leave," she said.

"Lock your door behind me," I said. "We don't want to take any chances, do we?"

She patted my cheek. "You're sweet, Harrison, but I'll be fine here on my own."

I left her to her restoration, and as I glanced back in once I was outside, she was already back at work. It made me feel somewhat better, realizing that I wasn't the only one wedded to my shop.

I drove to the bank and made my deposit, then thought about grabbing something to eat. Lately I'd been taking more and more of my meals alone, and I wondered if I was becoming some kind of recluse. It wasn't that I didn't enjoy being around people, but my time off alone was becoming precious to me. Still, At Wick's End was running smoothly, and I could afford a little socializing. I couldn't remember the last date I'd been on.

As I drove home, I wondered who I'd ask. At one time I would have said Heather might be a nice dinner companion, but lately, with her erratic actions and vanishing acts, I wasn't sure. The fact that she'd dated Aaron had nothing to do with it. Well, not a lot, at any rate. She'd reacted so strongly to his demise that I wondered how close they'd really been. It would most likely take her some time to get over him, especially since her chance at closure was now gone forever.

Erin? She intrigued me, there was no doubt about that, but I'd already asked her out once, and her reaction had been tepid, at best. Wow, I was certainly quite the ladies' man, wasn't I? Of one thing there was no doubt; I wouldn't go back to any of the women I'd dated casually before. It was time to meet someone new.

Saying it and doing it were two different things, though. I was past hanging out in bars, while I felt Laundromats and grocery stores were unacceptable singles' scenes, so that left customers at the shop and other tenants. Should I ask Sanora out? She was certainly lovely, and I did enjoy her personality. But she was also a suspect in her ex-husband's death, in my mind if not the police's. And if I was being honest with myself, Heather was, too, though I still had a hard time believing that. Tick was twenty years too old for me, Eve thirty years and too tempestuous to boot. Millie was married, so that brought me back to square one.

That was the way things seemed to go. Whenever I was looking, there was no one around, but the second I found myself starting a new relationship, the opportunities suddenly appeared boundless. I usually did fine on my own; I'd grown comfortable enough with my own company, but there were times when it would have been nice to have someone to call. It would happen again for me, but in the meantime, I did have plenty on my plate, certainly enough to keep me busy and occupied.

I was debating about what to make myself for dinner as I climbed the stairs to my apartment.

I couldn't have been more surprised to find Heather waiting for me by my front door.

Fourteen

I said, "Where have you been? What's going on with you? Do have any idea what's been happening around here?" My questions tumbled out in a rush.

"Slow down. Aren't you going to invite me in?"

"Of course I am." I stepped past her and unlocked the door to my apartment. "Come on in."

She followed me in, and I locked the door behind us. "Can I get you something to drink? How about a bite to eat?"

"No, I'm fine." She averted her gaze from me as she said solemnly, "Harrison, I didn't mean to run out on you like I did."

"You didn't run out on me, well, not just me. What happened?"

"I guess everything around here was just too much for me. First Aaron died, and then you sprang Sanora on me, it was more than I could take. So I left. That was a mistake."

The second she mentioned Sanora's name, a burning question came to mind. "Have you rented a truck lately for your move? A Wee Haul van, in particular?"

"What kind of a question is that?" she asked.

"One I need answered," I said.

She met my gaze and said solemnly, "No, I haven't rented a van, a Wee Haul or otherwise. I wouldn't leave without talking to you first."

So that cleared Heather of the attempted hit and run, at least if she was telling me the truth. Of course what would a little white lie count against trying to kill someone? On the face of it, her assurance shouldn't have meant a thing to me, but it did. I believed her, whether it was the right thing to do or not regardless of what Millie's husband George had heard about Heather renting a van.

I asked, "So what's going on in your life?"

She said, "It's been too crazy to tell. How are things at River's Edge?"

"Never a dull moment. Some genius tried to burn me out, somebody tried to run Sanora down with a van, and Pearly and Eve have been secretly dating."

She took it all in, then said, "So that's why you asked me about the van. I suppose I had that coming."

"Heather, I saw your sign change in the middle of the night and there was a rumor you were moving everything in your shop to Charlotte. You fired Mrs. Quimby, for goodness sake. What was I supposed to think?"

"I don't blame you, but I'd be lying if I said I wasn't disappointed that you didn't believe in me." She got up and started for the door.

"Wait a second, Heather, that's not fair. I never said a word to anyone but Millie."

"And what did she say?" Heather asked.

I admitted, "She didn't think you could do it, not for one second."

"So at least one of my friends still believes in me."

I said, "You haven't given me much reason to lately, but I believe in you, too. You can walk out of here right now, goodness knows you've done it before, but if you want to stay, you're welcome to."

She thought about it a second or two, then said, "You know what? You're right. I'm tired of running." She slumped down on the couch, then said, "If the offer's still open, I'll take that drink."

"You've got it. Is bourbon okay?"

"Cut it with some Coke," she said. I got the Maker's Mark out and poured her a drink, splashing some soda in on her request. Mine I took neat.

After she took a sip, she said, "Okay, you wanted to talk. I'm ready."

Suddenly I didn't have the heart to push her anymore. I was her friend, and though there were several questions I wanted to ask, our friendship had to come first. I said, "I'm not going to interrogate you. I do have one question, though."

"Fire away."

"Where's Esmeralda?" I asked.

Heather laughed. "I knew she'd get under your skin. She's got a way of making converts out of unbelievers."

I protested, "It's not that. I just wondered, that's all."

Heather said, "She's downstairs in my shop, curled up on her bed, if I know her. Don't worry, you can see her tomorrow."

I waved that off. The idea that I was getting close to her cat was ridiculous. I'd asked out of curiosity, nothing more. I thought about giving Heather the catnip mouse I'd picked up, but decided it could wait for another time.

I took a sip of my drink, then asked, "So are you staying, or did you come to say good-bye?"

"If you'll have me, I'm not going anywhere." There was a conviction in her words that I liked.

"As far as I know, your lease is still good."

She leaned forward and touched my knee. "That's not what I'm asking. If you don't want me here anymore, I'll pack up and move tomorrow."

I took a sip, then said, "Of course I want you here. You shouldn't even have to ask."

"Oh yes I should," she said. "Thank you, Harrison."

"For what?"

"For everything."

I smiled. "Well, I can't take credit for everything, but I'm happy to do my part. Are you sure you're going to be okay, working here with Sanora around?"

"I'm over it," she said. "I've had my little snit. I'm not saying we're going to be best friends, but I won't go out of my way to cross her."

"That's all I can ask for." I raised my glass to her, then said, "Welcome back."

"It's good to be back," she said.

I had a thought, one last thing to clear up in my mind while we were having a frank discussion. "Hang on a second," I said, "I'll be right back."

I retrieved the crystal bauble Sanora had discovered in Aaron's office and held it out to her. "I believe this belongs to you."

She studied it a second, then said, "Sorry, it's not mine."

"Are you sure?" I asked. "It looks like it came off a necklace or something."

She shook her head. "Nothing I carry. It looks like—."

At that instant, the outside lights sprang to life, shining through my window.

"Your security lights are working," she said.

I peered through the window. "I wonder who's out there at this hour." I was going to have to get Pearly to reposition the light over my apartment. There was a reflected glare that blinded me as I looked out.

"I'd better go see what's going on," I said, grabbing the baseball bat I kept by the door. "I'll be right back."

"I'm going with you," Heather said as she put her drink down.

"Maybe you should stay here," I insisted.

She just rolled her eyes. "Are you coming?" she said as she started for the door.

"At least let me lead the way."

I started to flip on the hall light when Heather put her hand on mine. "Maybe we shouldn't advertise that we're coming."

"That's a good idea," I said. There was enough light shining through for me to see the stairwell, and I grabbed the rail with one hand as I clutched the bat in the other. I had never been all that fond of guns, but the bat felt reassuring in my hand.

I carefully opened the door and found Sheriff Morton standing in front of Heather's shop.

"Have a night game?" he asked, then sneezed.

I relaxed. "Just thought we'd hit a few balls in the parking lot. I thought you were sick."

"No way," he said, then sneezed again. He looked as pale as I'd ever seen him.

I said, "No, you're a picture of perfect health. What are doing out here?"

Morton said, "Patrolling. Too many men out, so I had to work."

"Go home, sheriff. There's nothing going on out here."

He gestured to the lights. "Those are new."

"I thought they might help."

"Couldn't hurt," he said as he wiped at his eyes.

"Sheriff, if we need you, we'll call."

"Yeah, I'd better get back to the office."

I thought about offering to drive him, but decided against it, knowing that the only result of my offer would be his howling protest.

As he drove off, Heather came up behind me. I suddenly realized that she'd held back in the shadows as I'd spoken to the sheriff.

"There you are," I said.

"When I saw it was the sheriff, I went back for my purse. It's been a long day, and I want to get home."

I looked around and noticed her car was missing. "Where'd you park?"

"I'm in back. I'll just go through my shop and collect Esme, then I'm going home."

"Let me walk you through your store," I said.

"You don't have to," Heather protested.

"I know I don't have to. I want to."

As she unlocked the door to her shop, she said, "Admit it, you just want to say hi to the cat."

"Sure, that's it," I said as I followed her inside.

She flipped on a few lights as we entered the shop, and Esmeralda got up from her bed and stretched as only a cat could. I didn't expect her to rush to me, but we'd formed a friendship, so I thought she'd at least acknowledge my presence.

Instead, she ignored me utterly and jumped up into Heather's arms.

"Hello to you, too," I said.

Heather laughed. "What were you expecting? She's a cat, Harrison, not a dog."

"I know that," I said.

I walked her through her shop, then out the back. Heather put Esmeralda in the passenger seat and turned to me. She reached up on her tiptoes and kissed me on the cheek.

"What was that for?" I asked.

"For believing me."

I stayed there until she drove off, then walked back around to the front of River's Edge. I did believe her, whether I had reason to or not. Sanora was still a suspect, and so was Gary Cragg, but there was one person I'd ignored up to now: the mysterious Ms. X. It was time to track down Aaron Gaston's last love.

But it would have to wait until morning. I'd had a big day, and all I wanted to do was get some rest.

As I drifted off, I remembered the brush-off Esmeralda had given me. How could I begin to explain to a cat that the reason I hadn't seen her for so long had nothing to do with me? Maybe if I gave her the catnip mouse, she'd get over it.

Cats and women. I was no closer to understanding one of them than I was the other.

THE FIRST THING Eve noticed walking into At Wick's End the next day was the absent pair of candles. "What happened, did you finally decide to throw them out?"

I kept looking at my inventory sheet as I said, "No, I sold them after you left yesterday."

"You are kidding me," Eve said. "How in the world did you manage that?"

"I had a customer with very particular tastes."

She shook her head. "I don't believe it. Belle is probably spinning in her grave."

"Why do you say that?" I asked.

"Harrison, I can't believe she ever intended those for sale. They were her experiments, not her stock. She would have been appalled to have them go out the door."

"Then why did she put a price tag on them? A hefty one at that."

Eve asked suspiciously, "How much did you charge for them?"

When I told her, she started to smile, then her laughter followed. It was the first time since we'd been working together that I'd ever heard that particular sound coming from her.

I said, "Do you mind telling me what's so funny?"

After she settled down enough to speak, she said, "I was right. Belle never intended them to sell. That price tag was her way of insuring that they stayed."

"Well, he paid it without flinching." After her merriment, I wasn't about to admit that the customer who'd bought them had done so as a jibe and not a real gift.

"I suppose it's true after all. Taste is subjective."

I added, "It helped a rather lackluster day at that. How are you this morning?"

"I'm fine. Why do you ask? Have you heard something?"

"Easy," I said, "I was just checking."

She studied me a second, then said, "We have work to do."

"Hey, I'm not the one standing around," I admitted.

If I'd said it a few days earlier, she probably would have walked out on the spot. As it was, she clucked a few times, then said, "You're right. I'm getting busy right now." As she walked away, I heard her mutter to herself, "I can't believe anyone found them attractive."

I found myself diverting my step to the storeroom for the rest of day, intentionally missing the candles that weren't there anymore.

Millie visited At Wick's End ten minutes before we officially opened. She knocked on the door, holding two coffees and a bag in her hands.

I opened the door for her, then locked it behind her as one of my customers tried to follow her in. "We'll be open in ten minutes," I said.

"Then why does she get to go in now?" The woman asked plaintively in a definite Northern accent.

"Hey, what can I say? She brought me food."

The woman asked in all earnestness, "So if I bring you a chocolate cake tomorrow I can shop early?"

I said, "Ma'am, if you add milk-chocolate icing, I'll let you in half an hour before we officially open."

She shook her head as she said, "That's some way of running a business you've got there."

Millie called out, "Harrison, are you coming? I need to speak with you."

I nodded to my customer and locked the door. I should have let her in, but I wanted to talk to Millie without having to worry about being interrupted.

"What's going on?" I said as I took the coffee she offered. "Did you bring me a treat?"

"I'm trying a new recipe," she said, "and I thought you'd like to sample it."

"Always happy to help," I said as I reached for the bag.

"Harrison, that's not why I came by. Heather's back in her shop."

"I know," I said as I ate a lemon tart no bigger than my thumb. "I talked to her last night."

"Then you know Mrs. Quimby is leaving me. I don't know what I'm going to do, I've been so used to having her help in the mornings."

"Have you thought about asking her to stay part-time?" I asked. "Heather doesn't open till ten. That should take care of most of your morning rush and your lunch prep work."

She kissed my forehead. "What a grand idea. I'll go talk to her right now."

I unlocked the door for her and motioned my customer in, though it was still four minutes before I was scheduled to open. She glanced at her watch and said, "Are you certain? I don't even have any baked goods with me."

"I'm extending you credit on my cake," I said with a smile as I flipped the CLOSED sign to OPEN. She came in and Eve glanced sharply at me. I wasn't about to tell her about my humorous exchange.

"You can finish the order," I said. "I'll wait on her."

Eve scowled at me a second, then returned to her work.

After browsing through much of the store, the woman bought a healthy supply of new wax and a mold I'd special-ordered but had never been picked up by the customer.

She said, "I'm new here. You do things differently in the South, don't you?"

"You have no idea," I agreed. "Just wait till you've been here a while. We start to grow on you, I promise."

"That's what I'm afraid of," she said as she took the receipt I offered.

I gave her my best smile as I handed her the bag. "Trust me, in six months you'll never want to leave Micah's Ridge."

"We'll see," she said as she left.

I looked out in time to see Pearly walking past the store, but he never came in. After his third lap, I called out to Eve, "I'm going to step outside for a second. It's a beautiful day."

"Just don't wander off," Eve said. "We might get busy."

I looked around the empty store, glanced at the deserted parking lot, then said, "No, ma'am, I promise I'll be here for the rush."

I called Pearly's name, and he looked startled as he turned around to face me.

"Hello, Harrison."

"Are you going to pace out here all day? You're driving off my customers."

"Eh? Sorry, didn't mean to interfere," he said as he started to walk off.

"Hey, I'm only kidding. You're going to have to face her again sooner or later, you know that, don't you?"

"What are you talking about?"

"Come on, I'm not blind. I saw how she reacted to you. And remember, you already told me you were having trouble with your love life. It doesn't take a genius to figure out that Eve was one of your girlfriends." It felt odd calling my sixty-something employee a girl anything, but I was at a loss for what else to call her.

"That's just it. Eve's offended she wasn't on the list at all. Now I've really gone and done it."

I leaned against the brick of the building and said, "Let me get this straight. She's mad because you weren't two-timing her?"

"Three-timing, actually," Pearly admitted reluctantly.

"So what's the problem?"

Pearly said, "She asked me out two weeks ago, and I turned her down. I said I was too busy, and it was certainly the truth then. Harrison, let me ask you this? How in the world was I supposed to know she was in the same book club as the three women I was dating? Obviously if I'd had any idea they knew each other, I wouldn't have been so social."

I couldn't help it. As much as I sympathized with Pearly for his dilemma, I had to laugh. What a meeting they must have had when they'd discovered their connection.

"Any idea what book they were reading?" I asked.

Pearly said glumly, "I'm not going to tell you."

"Come on. I'm sorry I laughed. I know it's not that funny."

It took some prodding, but he finally said, "You won't stop hounding me until I tell you, will you?"

"If *you* don't tell me, I'll be forced to ask Eve," I said.

"Good gracious, don't do that. If you must know, they were reading *Death of a Ladies' Man*."

I was still laughing when he finally gave up on me and walked away in disgust.

Fifteen

I was just starting to think about lunch when Millie came in.

I said, "George is going to get jealous if you keep popping up here like this," I said.

"Oh posh, he's too busy to notice. I hope you haven't made any lunch plans."

"Is that an invitation? Now I'm starting to get ideas."

Millie blushed. "Can't a person do something nice for another? Of course, you're perfectly free to decline."

"No, ma'am, that wouldn't be very gentlemanly of me, now would it? May I ask what the occasion is? It's a good seven months till my birthday."

"It's my way of saying thank you for speaking with Heather. She told me you two had a long talk last night."

I glanced at Eve, who was taking every word in. I said to her, "I'll take the first lunch, if you don't mind."

"No bother," she said.

I led Millie outside. "Now she'll be on me the rest of the day."

"I thought Eve liked Heather," Millie said as we walked toward The Crocked Pot.

"Of course she does, but I can hear her now. 'Harrison Black, it's just not proper, having a young single woman in your apartment all hours of the night.' Man, oh man."

Millie started giggling. "I can hear her saying just that, though your delivery is a little off."

"That's the only thing that stood between me and a career in show business."

"What's that?" Millie asked.

"A severe lack of talent."

"Oh, Harrison."

Inside her café, one table by the window was roped off, and instead of the disposable plates and cups, this spot was set with fine bone china. I recognized the pattern. My grandmother had owned a complete set with the same baby roses.

"Wow, this is too much," I said. "Is this for me?"

Millie nodded happily. "I found this set at a yard sale, if you can believe it. Lovely, isn't it?"

"It's great," I said. "But there's only one place setting. I figured you'd be joining me."

"No time for that, I'm pretty busy." She lowered her voice and admitted, "Besides, I have just the one setting. That's why it was so cheap."

I sat down and Millie went in back for a minute. Though my first customer of the day had left my shop a couple of hours before, she must have lingered around River's Edge. She walked into The Crocked Pot, looked around and saw me sitting at the table, elegantly outfitted for a formal meal.

"Don't tell me," she said, "You do this every lunchtime."

I smiled. "Just every fifth Friday." It was the middle of the month, and decidedly not a Friday. She shook her head and said, "I suppose you have to get here early to understand things. Kindergarten is probably a good time."

"Don't bet on it. I've lived around here all my life, and

there are still some things I don't understand. That's what makes it so much fun."

Millie came out from the back, set a stainless steel covered tray in front of me and turned to the woman. "May I help you?"

"I don't have time for formal tea, or whatever is you're doing. Can I grab a cup of coffee to go?"

Millie looked puzzled by the exchange. "Of course you can." She wagged a finger at me. "Harrison, have you been telling stories again?"

"No, ma'am. But then how can you believe me? I might be lying right now," I added with a grin.

She shook her head and fixed the woman a coffee. After she paid, I heard her mumbling as she walked out. I didn't catch all of it, but it was something like, 'they're all mad as hatters' as she left. I held it in till she was gone, then laughed aloud.

As Millie approached my table with a covered plate, she said, "I don't even want to know."

I grabbed the lid and said, "May I?"

"It won't do you much good if you don't," she said.

I lifted the lid and found a slab of pot roast surrounded by golden braised carrots, red new potatoes, and silver onions. The smell alone was nearly enough to fill me up, it was so rich. "How did you know pot roast was my favorite?"

Millie smiled. "Believe it or not, your great-aunt told me."

"Belle talked about me?" I asked, suddenly forgetting all about the food, as wonderful as it smelled. I'd been more off than on with my great-aunt in the years before she died, and I just assumed it had been "out of sight, out of mind" between us.

"Belle and I spoke of a great many things, Harrison. It's only natural that her only kin would come up in the conversation now and then. She said you couldn't get enough pot roast growing up, that you'd turn down cherry pie for an extra slab of beef."

"What can I say, I know what I like." I surveyed the plate again, then said, "Honestly, you didn't have to do this."

"That's what made it so much fun. Now are you going to taste it or not?"

I took a forkful, watching as the meat fell apart at my touch. Adding a bite of carrot, a sliver of onion, and a chunk of potato, I had a full fork and a perfect bite.

"Well?" she asked.

"I can't describe it, it's so good," I said.

Millie smiled. "I'm glad you like it."

As a man in a business suit came in, Millie said, "Enjoy."

"May I help you?" she asked him.

"I was just coming in for a bagel, but I've changed my mind. I'll have what he's having. You can serve mine on a regular plate, I don't need anything fancy."

Millie smiled. "I'll have it ready in a minute."

The man loosened his tie, looked at me and said, "Is it as good as it smells?"

"Better," I said, then took another bite. For a minute I was afraid he was going to try to steal a carrot off my plate, but Millie came back soon enough. "Would you like coffee with that?"

"You wouldn't happen to have a tall glass of cold milk around, would you?"

"Coming right up."

He sat across the café, no doubt to enjoy his own memories. I watched him just long enough to see the expression on his face when he took the first bite, then returned my full attention to the meal before me.

Before I realized what I'd done, my plate was clean. "Seconds?" Millie asked.

"Not unless I take a nap for the rest of the day. I'm going to have a hard time staying awake as it is. Millie, that was wonderful."

"I'm so glad you enjoyed it. I thank you for talking to Heather."

"As I said, you're welcome. I'd say you shouldn't have, but I'd be lying. Now I'd better get back to work."

As I left the café, my blue jeans felt snug on me. I was going to have to do a lot more walking if I was going to be able to wear them much longer.

I lingered outside the candleshop, not eager to go back in on such a beautiful autumn day. There was that crispness in the air filled with a longing to cut school and play hooky. In the other jobs I'd had in my life, one day off now and then never made that much difference, and I probably took more time off than I should have. But if I was being honest with myself, there was a part of me that longed for those days. It wasn't that I didn't love At Wick's End, or River's Edge, for that matter, but I'd been in school entirely too long without a day off.

That wasn't going to happen, though.

I walked back in and found Eve watching me from the second I passed through our door.

I asked, "What is it? Did I get a stain on my shirt?"

She shook her head. "Not that I can see. Harrison, I've been meaning to talk to you."

Uh oh. This couldn't be good. "What's on your mind?"

"Don't you trust me?" she asked, a mixture of anger and hurt in her voice.

"What makes you ask me that? You know I do."

"Then why don't you ever take any time off? Believe it or not, the candleshop was running just fine before you came along. Belle used to take two afternoons off a week, and if the mood moved her, she would grab an entire day now and then, too. I'm perfectly capable of handling things around here."

"You know what? When you're right, you're right." I started for the door.

"Where are you going?"

I said, "I'm taking this afternoon off. After all, I trust you."

"I didn't mean right now," she said, surprised by the immediate success of her argument.

"There's no time like the present," I said. "See you in the morning."

"That will be fine," she said, still unsure about what exactly had happened.

I'd been looking for an excuse to get away, and Eve had offered me a perfect one.

I thought about going up to my apartment and changing, but my jeans would be good enough for whatever I wanted to do, and I honestly needed to get away from River's Edge.

There was gas in my truck, money in my wallet, and a smile on my face. I suddenly knew exactly what I wanted to do. I was less than an hour from the Blue Ridge Parkway, a place I truly loved. Who wouldn't? It was a ribbon of road that ran through some of the prettiest country there was. Even the forty-five-mile-an-hour speed limit appealed to me. I wanted time to savor the colors of the trees, and since the road wound through a higher elevation, I should get a great show. I would have never tried it on the weekend because of the traffic, but I figured I'd be safe during the week.

Driving up into the mountains, I rolled my windows down despite the chilly air and turned my radio off completely. It was an afternoon worth bottling, if I could have figured out a way to do it.

IT WAS NEARLY six by the time I got back to Micah's Ridge. Beside me on the seat, I had a bag of apples, a jug of cider, and a half a case of pumpkin butter. I was hooked on the stuff, and loaded up whenever I visited the mountains. It amazed me that I'd been able to get a week's worth of relaxation in one afternoon, and I promised myself to start taking advantage of having Eve there to run things at the candleshop. There was a world to see beyond the confines of At Wick's End, and I was going to start taking advantage of it.

Eve looked surprised to see me as I walked into the store. "Harrison, I thought you were gone for the day." She was totaling out the cash register and getting the deposit together.

"I know how much you hate going to the bank, so I thought I'd do it for you. Not that I don't trust you," I added with a smile.

I handed her a jar of pumpkin butter and said, "By the way, here's a souvenir from my trip."

I wasn't sure how Eve would react, but she smiled as she took the jar. "I haven't had this since I was a little girl."

"Well, then I'd say it's high time you had some now, wouldn't you say?"

She allowed a slight smile to break through. "You're certainly in a good mood, aren't you?"

"I appreciate the break," I said as she handed the deposit to me.

"Any time," she said.

"I'm going to hold you to that."

"Goodness me, I've created a monster."

I saluted her and said, "You can't even imagine."

I was feeling good about the world as I walked out of At Wick's End.

Then I heard angry voices down the way.

It appeared the truce between Sanora and Heather was officially over.

"I DON'T WANT you here," I heard Heather nearly shout as I rushed toward them.

"Do you honestly think I care what you want?" Sanora was matching her, toe to toe. "You tried to come between my husband and me. It didn't work, though, did it?"

Heather's cheeks burned. "He was your ex-husband."

"Ladies, what's going on?" I asked forcefully.

"Butt out, Harrison," Heather snapped.

"This doesn't concern you," Sanora added.

"So at least you two agree on something. This is all none of my business."

Neither one of them cracked a smile. Hey, it was a tough crowd.

I continued unabashed. "Since we've agreed it's a personal matter between the two of you, why don't we go somewhere in private where you can discuss the situation like adults."

"I'm not going anywhere with her," Heather said.

"I'm willing to," Sanora said, a little sweeter than needed.

Heather grunted at her, rolled her eyes at me, then stormed back into her shop.

I asked Sanora, "What brought that on?"

"I made the mistake of leaving my shop at the same time she left hers. Harrison, I'm not looking for trouble, but I won't be a doormat either."

"All I ask is that you two try to get along."

"You're talking to the wrong person then," Sanora said.

"Let me go talk to Heather. I'll see what I can do."

The wind chimes over Heather's door danced as I opened it, and she turned rigidly to me as I walked in.

"Harrison, I'm not in the mood for any foolishness right now, so just turn around and walk right back out."

Esmeralda lithely danced to me and leaped up into my arms. It looked like she'd forgiven me. "Sorry, I can't. I seem to have an armful of cat at the moment."

"How could you take her side like that?" Heather asked, the tears a heartbeat away.

"What are you talking about? I'm not taking anybody's side."

"Exactly," Heather crowed. "And why is that, Harrison? I thought we were friends. Apparently I was wrong."

I shook my head and scratched behind Esme's ear. She was purring contently as I did so. "If you think I'm some kind of fair-weather friend, you're sadly mistaken. But if you consider friendship me standing by while you muck things up, then you're wrong there, too. I'm trying to help, Heather."

"Then stay out of it," she said.

I laughed. "Sorry, that's not the kind of friend I am, either. I have a tendency to meddle. Probably should have told you that before, shouldn't I?"

She tried to look sternly at me, but my feigned sincerity won her over and her harsh countenance finally broke into a smile. "That's not fair. I want to be angry."

"By all means, don't let me stop you," I said.

"Why do you care, anyway?"

I said, "Well, you're my friend, and I want to help you get over this animosity you have for Sanora. Besides, things are tense around River's Edge, and it's not good for anyone. Any chance of burying the hatchet, and I don't mean in someone's back?"

"Oh, I won't sneak around to do it. I'll come at her from the front."

"Now, now, no backsliding. And here we were making such good progress."

She shook her head. "I admit it, I lost my temper. It won't happen again."

"So any chance we could offer her a cup of coffee and talk about it?"

Heather shook her head. "I've already talked too much as it is."

"Good enough. I do appreciate you making the effort."

I handed her Esme, who seemed reluctant to leave my grasp. "By the way, I believe this belongs to you."

She took her cat from me and gave me a genuine laugh. "Haven't you heard? Cats don't belong to people, it's the other way around."

I bowed to them both, then left while Heather was still in a good mood. I'd taken a chance, confronting them like that, then following up with Heather in her own den, but it had been true. Since Sanora's return, it felt as if all of River's Edge had been tiptoeing around the two of them. Maybe now they'd released enough tension to at least ignore each other if they couldn't manage civility.

I hoped so, at any rate.

The joy of my trip had been dampened but not entirely eliminated, so before anyone else had the opportunity to kill the rest of it, I decided to take the deposit to the bank.

Upstairs later, for dinner I had a few apples, sipped some cider, and had pumpkin butter on toast. That was one of the coolest things about being an adult, as far as I was concerned. Every now and then I could have dessert for dinner. Some people didn't think it was all that great a perk, but it was one I reveled in.

I was in no mood to go out.

Instead, I curled up with *Rest You Merry* from Ms. MacLeod and settled in for the night.

Sixteen

I normally got to At Wick's End an hour before opening the shop, but since I had indulged in a little extra sack time, I rolled in with just thirty minutes to spare.

I found the woman from the day before standing outside the door, a chocolate cake in her hands.

She offered it to me, then said, "Here's the cake, as promised."

I smiled broadly at her, trying to hide my surprise. My sense of humor oftentimes got me into trouble, but this was the first time it had brought me a cake!

"I see you've brought your golden ticket," I said as I unlocked the door and held it open for her.

She stepped inside, then said, "My husband thought you were kidding, but I knew better."

"You should have brought him along. I wouldn't have minded sharing."

She laughed. "Are you kidding me? He kept after me last night until I baked him one, too." I took the platter from her and said, "Feel free to look around. If you don't mind, I think I'll have a slice for breakfast."

"Breakfast? You're kidding me."

I shook my head. "Hey, it's got flour, eggs, all kinds of healthy stuff in it. Breakfast is the most important meal of the day, you know. Care to join me?"

"I had cereal, thanks anyway."

I smiled. "You don't know what you're missing." I flipped all the lights on and went back to the office for a knife, a couple of plates and two forks. I thought about trotting upstairs for a glass of cold milk, but since Eve wasn't due in until noon, I had to stay with the shop.

I put the utensils down and said, "Forgive me, but I should have introduced myself. I'm Harrison Black."

"Celeste DeAngelo," she said.

"Celeste, it's a pleasure knowing you." I cut a fat wedge of cake and tasted the first bite. "Wow, it's wonderful."

She smiled. "I'm glad you like it."

"Are you sure you won't join me? How about just a small slice?"

She laughed lightly. "Why not? I'll cut my own piece though."

I handed her the knife and she cut a sliver of cake and put it on the offered plate. I sneered at her serving size. "You could read through that. Come on, have some cake."

"This will do nicely," she said as she took a bite. "Bob will never believe this."

"I'm willing to bet if you offer him some for breakfast tomorrow, he won't say no."

She grinned. "No doubt you're right." We ate our cake, then Celeste said, "Now for some shopping."

I finished my slab, thought about getting another piece, then decided to wait until lunch. Dessert after lunch, I amended. I was going to have to supplement my menu with some healthy fare. And some time on one of Erin's kayaks, if I wanted to be able to wear my jeans much longer. Maybe if I worked it right I could slip out a little early. Well, Eve had opened the door for me taking more breaks from the shop. All I was doing was trotting through it.

Celeste picked out a nice array of things, from some beeswax blocks I'd just got to a Christmas-tree mold that I'd been wanting to try myself. I totaled her purchases up, then gave her a ten-percent discount.

"Why the price break?" she asked as she saw the minus sign on the register.

"Didn't I tell you? It's chocolate-cake day. Hey, they're a lot better than coupons."

She thanked me, then walked out just as it was time to officially open up. "Come back soon, Celeste, and you don't have to bring a cake with you next time."

"Don't tell me, you'd like an apple pie next, wouldn't you?"

"Well, I wouldn't say no to one, but you don't have to bake something every time you come."

"Come on, Harrison, don't let me down and start getting normal on me. My friends back home are going to howl about this."

I shuddered when I thought about what new stereotypes about the South I was setting, but let them think we were all a bunch of eccentrics. It was my bit as goodwill ambassador for the land below the Mason-Dixon line.

I'D NEARLY FORGOTTEN about my next session with Mrs. Jorgenson when Eve came in at noon and reminded me. She said, "Are you ready?"

"Ready for what?" I asked. "I'm not going to lunch today." I'd had another piece of cake midmorning, despite my good intentions, and I was still pretty full.

"Good, you could probably use the practice. She's due here in less than an hour."

Then it hit me. "Thanks, I forgot all about it. Don't worry, I'll be ready."

I left Eve to manage the front and started making preparations for my next lesson in candlemaking. If Mrs. Jorgenson arrived promptly, which I had no doubt she would, I'd have just enough time to dip the demonstration candles for today's lesson. That was the thing with Mrs. Jorgenson; she always wanted to start from the ground up, but once she'd mastered a technique, she was perfectly happy to let me do the grunt work in preparation. And why not? She was paying handsomely for the privilege, money the candleshop could ill afford to lose.

We'd done translucent candles during our last session, so I decided on a nice, warm red for our candles today. On a lark, I set up two double-boilers with melting wax, then changed the hue just enough to see the difference between the two pots.

I knew I could set my watch by her. Just as the first batch of candles were cooling from their dips, Mrs. Jorgenson rushed into the room.

"Sorry I'm late," she said.

I glanced at the clock and realized that she was two minutes past due. "I was about to give up on you," I said with a smile.

She didn't notice. "I don't expect you to extend the lesson on my account."

"Hey, it's on the house. I'll even throw in a piece of chocolate cake at the end."

"I don't eat chocolate, and I haven't had cake since my seventh birthday."

I should have known better than try to tease with her. Though she'd warmed up to me since we'd started our lessons, we weren't exactly at the "buddy" stage.

She looked disappointed when she saw the dipped pairs of candles on the racks. "I thought I'd be doing that today."

"I figured if I skipped the first few steps we could get right on it. After all, you've mastered dipping."

She nodded, then said, "Yes, I suppose you're right, but I do enjoy it so. Will we be twisting tapers again today?"

"No, ma'am, we're going to the next stage and start braiding candles. It's great fun."

"What do we do first?" she said, eager to get started.

"It's the same basic technique, we just add one more candle and braid the three together."

She selected two of the darker red tapers and one of the lighter, then braided them with expert skill. "You've been practicing," I said.

"I may have made a twist or two since our last lesson."

"No braiding?" I asked.

She said, "Not candles, at any rate."

"Let me guess, you used to braid your sister's hair." No matter how hard I tried, I couldn't see Mrs. Jorgenson as a little girl. Some people were just born middle aged.

"No, but the late Mr. Jorgenson used to enjoy braided loaves of bread and it's the same principal, isn't it?"

"You never talk about him," I said. "What was he like?"

For a minute I thought she wasn't going to answer. After some hesitation, she said, "He was jolly, and he had a way of making me laugh as well. He also had a gift of acquiring money that was quite astounding, though I told him repeatedly I would have rather had the time he stole from us than all the money in the world." She suddenly realized how much she was revealing and said, "Are you going to braid those, or may I?"

"They're all for you," I said.

I'd thought I had made too many tapers for the lesson, but Mrs. Jorgenson used them all. "It's amazing how they touch and then separate again, isn't it?"

"It is."

She held one braid she was particularly proud of and

said, "I know I'm just a silly old woman, but would you accept this as a way of my saying thank-you above and beyond my regular payment? Look at me, giving a candle to a candlemaker."

She started to pull it away, but I wouldn't let her. "I'm honored," I said as I took it. "I'll start burning it tonight."

She looked pleased by my acceptance.

After Mrs. Jorgenson was gone, Eve said, "What was that all about?"

"I'm not quite sure I know myself," I said.

Eve glanced at the clock, then said, "I don't want you to think I'm trying to get rid of you, but if you'd like, I'd be happy to watch the shop for the rest of the day."

"I can't do that to you," I said. "I've been taking too much time off lately as it is."

"Please, Harrison, you're here all the time. It's only two hours until closing. Go."

"You've talked me into it," I said. "I'll be back for the deposit, though."

"It can wait until tomorrow. See you then."

" 'Bye, Eve. And thanks."

"At Wick's End belongs to you. I'm just trying to get you to enjoy it a little more."

I thought about going by Erin's for a kayak ride, but then I remembered I owed Wayne a call, and a tennis match, if he was up for it. Wayne was a great deal more to me than my mechanic; he was also one of my best friends in the world. But lately, since taking over River's Edge, I'd been too busy to do anything with him, and finally he'd stopped asking. He was one part of my old life I didn't want to change.

I went up to my apartment and dialed the phone number to his garage.

When I got him on the line, he said, "Wait a second, the voice sounds familiar. Don't tell me, give me a second, I'll get it."

"You are such a funny guy. Any chance you can skip out early and get a few sets of tennis in?"

"What happened, did the candleshop burn down?"

"Bite your tongue. No, I thought I'd take a few hours off. We could hit some balls."

"I don't know," he said. "Let me check my schedule."

I waited a few minutes, then he came back on. "Nothing here that can't wait. My guys have it under control. You want to meet me at the court?"

"See you in half an hour."

I changed into shorts and a long-sleeved T-shirt, grabbed my racket and a can of balls I'd had three months, and headed out. When I got to the court, Wayne pulled up right behind me.

I said, "Perfect timing. How have you been?"

He shook my hand in a grip that could have broken every finger if he'd wanted to. "I've been busy, but that's a good thing. You ready?" he asked after we both stretched a little.

"A moment of silence," I said, as a part of our ritual. We both stood there as I peeled back the lid of the can, and I was rewarded with the swoosh of air as the seal was broken.

I tossed a ball to him, took two for myself, then jogged over to the other side of the court. My serve was rusty, but I managed to get one in after three straight shots into the net.

The only silver lining was that Wayne hadn't played since the last time we'd taken the court together either.

WE SPLIT THE first two sets and were both too tired to play a third. Wayne reached in the back of his truck and brought out a cooler.

"Want one?" he asked as he brought out a bottle of water.

"Sure," I said and we moved to a picnic table nearby.

As we drank, Wayne asked, "So how's life among the flames?"

"I lost a tenant at River's Edge."

He nodded. "That's right, I read about that potter in the paper. Some freak accident, right?"

"I don't think so. You don't want to hear about it, do you?"

Wayne said, "Are you kidding? The most exciting thing that's happened to me lately is that I worked on Sandra Bullock's car. At least she looked like her until I got closer. Give."

So I told him about Aaron's death and the suspects in my mind. "The lawyer did it," he said flatly.

"Why do you think that?"

"Why not? They're always up to something no good."

I shook my head. "As foolproof as your logic is, I don't think so."

He said, "Sounds like Aaron was a bit of a player."

"That's the way it's turning out, but I never would have pegged him for one."

Wayne took a drink of his water, then said, "So who's the last woman in his life?"

"I'm not sure," I admitted.

"You might want to find out."

"Why do you say that?"

He polished off his water, then said, "Think about it. He's had an ex-wife for quite a while, and unless you think this Heather did it, you've got to look at his last love. Especially since you won't agree with me about the lawyer. Follow his love life."

"How do I find out who she was? He was keeping this one a secret, as far as I can tell."

"Somebody had to have seen her visit him. Ask your other tenants."

I laughed. "You been watching *Murder, She Wrote* again?"

"Hey, you asked."

"No, you're right. I'm going to see if I can figure this out."

Wayne said, "When you do, let me know. This is frustrating. It's like reading a book and finding out the last chapter is missing."

"Books are neat; it's life that's messy," I said.

"Get that out of a fortune cookie, did you?"

I slapped him on the back. "Do me a favor, buddy, don't ever change."

He held his hands out. "Why should I? I'm the perfect me."

As I drove back to River's Edge, I wondered if anyone had seen Aaron's secret love. It wouldn't hurt to ask around.

AFTER A SHOWER and changing into clean clothes, I had just enough time to talk to Millie before she left for the day. Unfortunately, she hadn't seen a soul. Nor had Tick, or Heather, or any of the other first-floor tenants, though Heather suggested I talk to Sanora.

I was going to do just that, but The Pot Shot was closed when I went by. So it was another dead end.

When I got up to my apartment, there was something taped to my door. For a second I thought Markum might be back in town. Then I saw the words. "Mind your own business or else."

It appeared that someone wasn't happy with me.

Most likely Heather or Sanora had decided I was being too nosy butting into their business, but I thought the note was over the top. I started to throw it away when I got inside, then thought better of it and put it on the table by the door. Tomorrow I'd have to ask them about it and see if I could mend fences. With all of us working so closely together at River's Edge, I didn't want something like this hanging over our heads.

I put the water on to boil, sincne tonight was going to be spaghetti night given the state of my finances, and then I set the table. The center of it looked bare, so I searched around for a candle to burn. It was a habit I'd started with Belle's tribute soon after she'd died, and I'd found it soothing.

I spotted the braided candle Mrs. Jorgenson had given me and decided to light it for my companionship. The braided wicks, overdipped a few times to make them one piece, lit readily as the candle began to burn.

By the time the pasta was ready and the sauce heated, the three candles had burned enough to separate slightly before rejoining. What a wonderful gift from my star student.

The pasta was good, though the sauce was a little sweet for my taste. I blew the braided candle out, then curled up on the couch to finish my book. For once, I was able to spend a quiet evening alone at River's Edge.

I was in dire need of it, even if it did turn out to be the calm before the storm.

Seventeen

"I need to speak with you," I said the next morning as I saw Heather going into her shop. I'd been watching out for her since I'd come down, the note weighing heavily on my mind.

"What's up?" she asked as she walked in ahead of me. I followed her, then said, "Do you happen to know anything about this?"

She took the note from me and read it, then shoved it back at me. "It looks like Sanora didn't take too kindly to your interference yesterday."

"So you didn't write this?"

"You've got to be kidding me. How long have we known each other, Harrison? If I felt this way, do you honestly think I'd write you a note?"

"Of course not," I said. "Not if I was around to yell at," I added with a grin.

"Exactly. Go talk to Sanora."

The potter was outside in front of her shop displaying some small pieces on a table.

"Aren't you afraid somebody will steal these pieces?" I asked.

"From my bargain table? They're welcome to them, if they're that desperate. I put my culls out here, marked down of course, then if they like what they see, it brings them inside. You should try it with some of your candles."

"It sounds like a good idea," I admitted.

"So is that why you're here, looking for retailing tips?"

I shook my head. "It's about this."

She didn't even touch it, but read it in my hands. "My goodness, you certainly made Heather mad yesterday. You should talk to her about it. Look how hard she wrote the letters. The paper's even torn in a place or two."

"So you didn't write it either, then."

She frowned. "Of course not. I'm an adult, Harrison. If I have a problem with you, you won't find out about it from a note, believe me."

"Heather denies writing it, too. So if you didn't write it, and she didn't, who did?"

Sanora said jokingly, "Who else have you offended lately? For a candlemaker, you certainly do cultivate trouble, don't you?"

"More than I ever imagined," I said as I excused myself and headed back to At Wick's End. If Sanora and Heather were both telling the truth, then I had offended someone else with my meddling. Could one of the other tenants have resented my inquiries the day before? Or was this about something else entirely? If it involved Aaron's murder, then I'd struck closer to home than I'd realized. If I only knew which arrow had hit its mark.

In the meantime, I decided to take Markum's advice a little more seriously than I had up to then. It was time to start watching my back.

I found Cragg in his office after my lunch break and decided to show him the note as well.

"And you think I wrote this," he said after examining it.

"I don't think anything. I'm just asking."

"If I ever decide to write you, it will be in the body of a lawsuit," the attorney said.

There wasn't much room for doubt in that, either.

I went through the rest of the day at the shop, but Eve would have probably been better off if I had called in sick. I couldn't get the warning out of my mind, wondering what it meant.

She said, "Harrison, I need your key to the back door. Mine is at home."

"Sorry, what was that, Eve?"

She shook her head. "Honestly, what world are you in? Let me borrow your key to the back, I need to get to the dumpster."

I fished into my pockets and pulled out my keys, bringing out the crystal piece Sanora had found in her shop along with them.

"That's pretty," Eve said, spying it. "What is it?"

"I'm not quite sure," I said as I handed her the keys.

Eve said, "Can I trust you to wait on our customers while I'm throwing out those boxes?"

"I'm fine."

A customer came in while Eve was throwing out the trash, and I found myself debating the merits of stearins versus releases with him by the time she came back. The rest of the day passed quickly enough, though I was no closer to the truth than I had been earlier. At least I'd sold a fair amount of supplies and candles, enough to make my nut for the day, at any rate. I was going to have to leave the detecting to Sheriff Morton and stick to what I knew.

PAYDAY WAS THE next day, and I'd managed to spend my last check completely, even given my free rent and utilities. It was sandwiches tonight, but I promised myself steak the next night.

Though the meal wasn't all that formal, I lit the braided candle again and watched it burn as I ate. There was something about the way the lights brightened when the wicks burned together, then lessened as they separated. I felt in my pocket for the piece of quartz and held it up to the candlelight. Light danced through the facets, throwing off a glow that intensified the candle's output.

Suddenly I knew where the piece had come from. And unless I missed my guess, I had a good idea who had dropped it in Aaron's shop. Following the logic of all I'd seen and heard, that led me to the murderer. I thought about confronting the killer, but decided to call the sheriff instead. It was his job, after all, to take the risks.

He was singularly unimpressed with my detective work. "Harrison, I've got a fever and a case of the trots. I'm not getting dressed and driving all the way over there at night based on one of your wild theories."

"Will you at least come by in the morning?"

"We'll see," he said and hung up.

I wasn't about to wait until morning, though. While the killer was away, I was going to do a little detective work on my own. Maybe if I had more hard evidence by morning, Morton would be more inclined to listen to me.

I pulled the key I needed off Pearly's board in the maintenance room, glad I'd insisted on having the key to that area myself. What I was doing was probably breaking and entering, but if I happened to be caught in the act of snooping, I was all ready with my story. I was going to claim that I'd smelled something burning and had investigated before calling the fire department.

I wasn't eager to be caught, though. Before I entered the shop in question, I went by the candleshop and grabbed a taper. Overhead lights would surely give me away, and even a flashlight could be suspect, but I was betting that a shielded candle wouldn't be that easily seen from the outside.

I unlocked the door, glad my tenant didn't have an alarm system, and started exploring the shop. I was about to give up after an hour's search, failing to match the piece in my pocket with anything there.

Then I stumbled across its mates in the workshop in back. Holding the piece of crystal up to the desk lamp, I knew in an instant it was a perfect match.

Then the overhead lights came on, nearly blinding me with their intensity.

"Harrison, what are you doing stumbling around in here in the dark?"

"I thought I smelled something," I said.

"If that were true, you would have turned on the lights." A look of quiet desperation softened the hard edges of her face. "You know, don't you?"

"I don't know what you're talking about."

She pulled a gun from her purse almost reluctantly, and I could see the scrolls and curlicues on the barrel.

Tick said, "It's an antique, like everything else in my shop, but let me assure you, it works perfectly."

The candle in my hand started to shake as I saw Tick's finger start to tighten on the trigger.

"CAN I AT least know why?" I asked, hoping to buy a little time.

"Come now, there won't be any rescuers tonight, Harrison. You ask why? Aaron destroyed my heart. He honestly thought he could cast me away like some bauble he grew tired of playing with."

"But why go after Sanora? What did she do to you?"

"Are you talking about the hit and run? Happenstance, Harrison, purely an accident, and one I had nothing to do with. How delightful it would have been if it had happened though. I'm not a fan of Sanora's. She and Aaron talked about everything, or so she told me. However, my name somehow never came up, if Sanora is to be believed. I was home free until you started nosing around."

"Why write that note? I don't understand that."

She said, "That was foolish of me. I'm not prone to acting rash, but you visited my shop, and you suddenly seemed to take an interest in me, so I panicked."

"I was just trying to get to know you better," I said.

"Oh, Harrison, I'm truly sorry about this," she said as her finger started to tighten on the trigger.

Behind her, we both heard the sneeze at the same time. Her gun went from me to the sheriff.

"Drop it," Morton said. Without taking his eyes of her, he said, "I knew you couldn't leave it alone, Harrison." He said to her, "Give up."

"I hardly think so," Tick said. "I'll have to do some staging, but I think I can make this work. You shot Harrison thinking him a prowler, and he shot you thinking the same."

"It's not going to work out that way," Morton said.

"Oh, I think it is."

I didn't want anyone shooting anyone else. I had an idea. Tick had told me once of her fear of fire, and I still had a lit candle in my hand. I threw it at her, hoping that she wouldn't squeeze off a shot by accident, and was rewarded with a direct strike of flames in the mass of her hair. It caught fire from the hairspray and she dropped the gun as she beat out the fire with her hands. I grabbed a soda from her workbench and poured the remnants out on her head, effectively quenching the fire. After we were certain it was out, Morton cuffed her and led her away.

"Can you come down to the police station?" Morton asked after he blew his nose. "I need to interview you."

"I'm right behind you," I said.

Tick never said another word as he led her away.

* * *

THE NEXT DAY, I made a sign that said, CLOSED FOR GOOD and put it in Tick's window. Millie saw me doing it and said, "I heard what happened. I can't imagine all that happening right under our noses."

I said, "You never know about people, do you?"

"Poor Aaron," she said. "He wasn't a prince, not by any means, but he deserved better than he got."

"He crossed the wrong woman, there's no doubt about that," I said.

Sanora and Heather approached together, and it looked like the two of them were starting to patch up their differences.

"Harrison," Sanora said, "Thank you."

"Are you two friends now?" I asked.

"Let's just say we're making an effort to leave the past where it belongs," Heather said. "After all, we both loved the same man at one time in our lives, even if he wasn't perfect."

"It's a start," Sanora said. "What's going to happen to the shop?"

I groaned and said, "It looks like I'm going to have to find another tenant."

Millie said, "I've got a friend in Hickory who would be perfect for us. As a matter of fact, I'm going to go call her right now. Why don't you all join me at The Crocked Pot? Coffee and doughnuts are on me."

"Why not?" Sanora said as Heather nodded her agreement.

"I'll be there in a second," I said as I bolted Tick's door shut.

I went back to the candleshop and finished my display in the window first. It featured one of Mrs. Jorgenson's fanciest four-taper braids in the center of it, and the steps to making it all around.

It was the least I could do, since her candle had helped show me the way. Four lives had touched at different times; Aaron's, Heather's, Sanora's, and Tick's; burning separately, together, and then all apart again as time passed.

And now one of the tapers had been extinguished forever.

Candlemaking Tips
and Fun with Dipped Candles

Dipped candles, sometimes called tapers, can be great fun, and once you've mastered the basic technique there are lots of variations to experiment with. After your melted wax reaches the proper temperature, the layers build up on your wick at a satisfying pace; but be careful, that wax is hot! Each dip of the wick builds another layer on the growing candle, and before you know it, you've made your very own taper. You can add scents and dyes to your wax, and make lots of different sizes, too. Sometimes I like to make small tapers the size of birthday candles for fun.

One of my favorite things to do with a freshly-dipped candle is to twist it. The wax needs to be warm and flexible for this technique, so it works best on a brand new candle. Take the warm candle and place it on a hard surface, then use an old rolling pin to flatten the middle part of the candle. You need to press firmly here to get the wax flat enough for a pretty twist. The flattened section should be about half an inch thick after it's rolled out. Pick the candle up, grasp the top edge of the flat section with one hand and the bottom of the flattened area with the other. Work quickly here, because the wax is cooling. Gently twist the candle into a spiral until you've got a shape you like, kneading it as you go along.

Another fun thing to do with freshly-dipped candles is to braid them, just like Harrison and Mrs. Jorgenson do in the book. Take two or three freshly-dipped candles and put them on a flat surface. Then, starting from the bottom, plait them into a braid as you go. It's as easy as that. Squeeze the candles together gently before they cool, then check the bottom to make sure it fits into a candleholder.

These candles are beautiful to burn, if you can bring yourself to do it! Don't worry, though; the great thing about candlemaking is that you can always make more.

Have fun, and don't be afraid to experiment.

Happy candlemaking!

Cranberry Muffins

I'm a big fan of muffins like Millie makes,
especially cranberry ones around the holidays.
This recipe is simple to use and fills your kitchen with
a wonderful aroma as well as yielding baked treats that taste great.

1 egg
3/4 cup milk
1/2 cup vegetable oil (I like to use canola)
3/4 cup cranberries, halved
2 cups all purpose flour
1/3 cup sugar
3 teaspoons baking powder
1/2 teaspoon salt

This recipe makes about a dozen muffins. I like to use cupcake sleeves in my muffin pan to make cleaning up easier. Heat your oven to 400 degrees. Beat the egg, then stir in the milk and the oil. After that, add the cranberry halves to the liquid. Mix the dry ingredients together, then add them to the liquid, using a sifter. Stir just enough to moisten the flour, and don't worry if the batter is a little lumpy. Fill the cups about halfway to three quarters full. You can sprinkle the tops with sugar before you put them in the oven if you like them a little sweeter. Bake until the muffins are golden brown—about 20 minutes should do it—then enjoy.

AUTHOR BIOGRAPHY

Tim Myers lives with his family near the Blue Ridge Mountains he loves and writes about. He is the award-winning author of the Agatha-nominated Lighthouse Inn mystery series, the Candlemaking mystery series, as well as over seventy short stories.

Tim has been a stay-at-home dad for the last thirteen years, finding time for murder and mayhem whenever he can.

To learn more, visit his website at www.timmyers.net or contact him at timothylmyers@hotmail.com

First in the
Candlemaking Mystery
series by

Tim Myers

At Wick's End

Includes candlemaking tips!

Harrison Black has to learn the art of
candlemaking fast when he inherits his
Great-Aunt Belle's shop, At Wick's End.
But when someone breaks into the
apartment Belle left him, Harrison begins
to suspect that her death may not have
been an accident.

0-425-19460-4

**Available wherever books are sold or at
www.penguin.com**

pc894